"So, you do w ... **Rachel said**

Gabriel put out his hand and wiped a smudge of moisture from her lip with his thumb. "There's no harm in wishing, is there?"

Rachel's breathing quickened. "I don't believe this."

"Why not?" Gabriel's lips twisted. "Because you can't imagine us in bed together?" He made a small sound of regret. "Obviously your imagination is not as vivid as mine."

But it was, thought Rachel unhappily. She could imagine them in bed together only too well.

ANNE MATHER has been writing since she was seven, but it was only when her first child was born that she fulfilled her dream of becoming a published author. Her first book, *Caroline,* met with immediate success and since then Anne has written more than 130 novels, reaching a readership that spans the world.

Born and raised in the north of England, Anne still makes her home there with her husband, two children and, now, grandchildren. Asked if she finds writing a lonely occupation, she replies that her characters always keep her company. In fact, she is so busy sorting out their lives that she often doesn't have time for her own! An avid reader herself, she devours everything from sagas and romances to suspense.

A *New York Times* bestselling author, Anne Mather has also seen one of her novels, *Leopard in the Snow,* turned into a film.

Anne Mather

A RICH MAN'S TOUCH

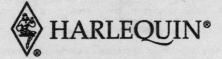

HARLEQUIN®

TORONTO • NEW YORK • LONDON
AMSTERDAM • PARIS • SYDNEY • HAMBURG
STOCKHOLM • ATHENS • TOKYO • MILAN • MADRID
PRAGUE • WARSAW • BUDAPEST • AUCKLAND

ISBN 0-373-12230-6

A RICH MAN'S TOUCH

First North American Publication 2002.

Copyright © 2001 by Anne Mather.

This edition published by arrangement with Harlequin Books S.A.

® and TM are trademarks of the publisher. Trademarks indicated with
® are registered in the United States Patent and Trademark Office, the
Canadian Trade Marks Office and in other countries.

Visit us at www.eHarlequin.com

Printed in U.S.A.

CHAPTER ONE

'Hey, isn't that Gabriel Webb sitting over there by the window? Wow!' Stephanie's eyes were wide with speculation. 'What's he doing in here? Slumming?'

'Do you mind?' Rachel bent to take a tray of golden-brown scones from the oven, hoping her friend would attribute her reddening face to the heat emanating from the cooker. 'Coming into my café is not slumming!'

'Oh, you know what I mean,' exclaimed Stephanie ruefully, tying the ends of her apron about her waist. 'But I've never seen him in here before, have you?' She grimaced. 'You have to admit, Rachel's Pantry is not his usual hangout.'

'I don't know where he usually has his morning coffee,' retorted Rachel, refusing to admit that she had spent the last twenty minutes wondering much the same thing herself. 'So long as he pays his bill. That's all that matters.'

Stephanie gave her friend a wry look. 'Oh, right. And it doesn't concern you at all that he should choose to come into this particular café. I mean, Kingsbridge is not a big place, I know, but it does have a couple of good hotels, and I know for a fact that when any of the executives from Webb's Pharmaceuticals are in town they usually stay at the County.' She glanced surreptitiously over her shoulder. 'What did he say?'

'I haven't spoken to him,' said Rachel shortly. 'Patsy took his order.'

'Which was?'

'Oh, for heaven's sake, Steph!' Rachel gazed at her friend with disbelieving eyes. 'A pot of tea, if you must know. There: are you satisfied now?'

'Tea!' Stephanie cast another glance towards the occupant of the window table. 'Not coffee?'

'Tea,' repeated Rachel in a low, forbearing tone. 'Now, do you mind starting on the lasagne? It's going to be lunchtime before we know where we are.'

'Okay, okay.' Stephanie held up her hands in mock submission. 'I'm starting right now.' She turned to take a pile of dishes from the shelf behind her. 'And I'm sorry if I'm a bit late but I ran into Mrs Austen in the High Street and she couldn't wait to tell me all about her trip to see Mark and Liz in Australia. I couldn't shut her up, honestly, Rach. According to her, they've got this really lovely house in a Sydney suburb, and Mark's going into business with someone who makes power boats, jet skis, that sort of thing.' She glanced at her friend as she started unfolding sheets of pasta. 'Pretty exciting, huh?'

'What? Oh, yes.'

Rachel managed a suitable response, but in all honesty she hadn't really been listening to what the other woman was saying. Despite her protestations to the contrary, she was supremely conscious of Gabriel Webb's presence, and the uneasy suspicion that perhaps he had come here to talk about Andrew couldn't be denied.

Her lips tightened. Surely that was ridiculous. She hadn't seen Andrew for over a year. As far as she knew he was living in London, and although she'd heard recently that his father had come back to the mansion the Webbs owned in Kingsbridge, she hadn't associated his return with herself.

Nor did she wish to, she acknowledged grimly. Andrew had hurt her, in more ways than one, and she wanted nothing more to do with him or his family. His mother was dead, of course, but if Gabriel Webb had some idea about warning her not to try and contact his precious son again, he was wasting his time. Rachel had no intention of letting the younger man back into her life.

'So how long has he been there?'

Stephanie's head was bent over her task but Rachel knew exactly who she was talking about. However, she didn't intend to get involved in another discussion about Gabriel Webb, and, being deliberately obtuse, she said, 'About five years, I think. He and Liz emigrated the year after Hannah was born. Did Mrs Austen say if she had any grandchildren yet?'

Stephanie turned her head. 'Oh, very funny,' she exclaimed. 'You know I wasn't talking about Mark Austen. What is it with you? Are you afraid of the man or something?'

'Afraid of Gabriel Webb?' Rachel's face suffused with colour. 'Of course I'm not afraid of him. I just don't understand what all the fuss is about. He's just another customer, for God's sake! Just because I once dated his son—'

'You make it sound like a one-night-stand,' protested Stephanie, sprinkling cheese on top of the pasta. 'You and Andrew went out together for months. Everybody thought he was serious about you until his father got heavy and broke you two up.'

'It wasn't—'

Rachel bit off her words before she said something she shouldn't. It had been easier to let her friends think that Gabriel Webb had split them up than admit that Andrew had been to blame for the breakdown of their relationship. Kinder, too—to herself as well as Hannah, she conceded bitterly. No way had she been willing to involve her daughter in that sorry mess, and she had no doubt that Andrew's father's relief would have been as great as his son's.

'I'd rather not talk about it,' she said at last, aware that Stephanie was waiting for her to finish her sentence. 'Oh, Patsy.' She turned with some relief to the teenager who had just returned from clearing tables. 'Can you clear these dishes away, please? And then go and ask—that gentleman by the window if he wants anything else.'

'Okay.'

Patsy was a willing helper and Rachel hoped her intervention had put an end to Stephanie's gossip. Her eyes flickered reluctantly towards her unwelcome customer and then, squashing any doubts that still lingered, she took down the menu board to amend the day's specials.

'How much do I owe you?'

His voice was low and attractive, deeper than Andrew's had been and possessing a warm sensuality that prickled Rachel's startled nerves. Despite the fact that she had gone out with his son for several months, Andrew had never introduced her to his family. And although most people in Kingsbridge knew who Gabriel Webb was, apart from seeing his picture in newspapers and magazines, this was the first time Rachel had seen him face-to-face.

Her mouth dried. This close, she realised he was younger than she'd imagined. Probably mid-forties, she guessed, though he didn't look well. His dark hair, which was shorter than his son's had been, was liberally spliced with grey, and there were dark rings around eyes that were so dark as to appear almost black in this light. She wondered if he'd been ill and then chided herself for even caring. Just because there were hollows in his cheeks and his clothes hung on his lean, angular frame, he wouldn't welcome her sympathy. Wouldn't welcome anything from her—or her daughter.

'I—' Aware that Stephanie was probably listening to their every word, Rachel wished she could just tell him it was on the house and ask him to leave. But after spending the last few minutes trying to convince her friend that his presence didn't bother her, she had to try and behave as if she had complete control of the situation. 'Um—one ninety-five, please.'

'One ninety-five?' He nodded. 'Right.' He fumbled in the pocket of his trousers and came out with a five-pound note. He put it on the counter and turned away. 'Thank you.'

'Wait!' Rachel wanted no charity from him. And when he turned to see why she had spoken she held up her hand.

'Your change,' she said, ringing the money into the till and extracting the necessary amount. 'You forgot your change.'

'I didn't forget,' he said flatly, heading for the exit, but Rachel went after him. Ignoring the fact that Stephanie was now staring after her with a look of disbelief on her face, she went round the counter and caught up with him at the door.

'The service charge is included,' she told him tightly, holding out the money. 'If you'd wanted to leave a tip, you should have given it to Patsy.'

Gabriel Webb's gaunt face wore a resigned expression as he took the coins from her. 'Is this necessary?' he asked, and she was relieved that he spoke so quietly that even Stephanie's sharp ears could not have heard his words. 'I realise you probably don't like me, Rachel, but I'd have thought you might control your antagonism for the sake of your staff.'

Rachel was taken aback. Not just by his use of her name but by the fact that he evidently had expected her antipathy. 'I don't know you, Mr Webb,' she declared when she could find her tongue, and he inclined his head.

'No, you don't,' he conceded drily. 'Which is why you might have given me the benefit of the doubt.' Thick lashes veiled the glitter of those dark eyes. 'I am sorry if you think my intention was to offend you. It wasn't.' His shoulders moved in a dismissive gesture. 'But anyway, if I did, my apologies.'

Rachel took an involuntary backward step. There was something about him that disturbed her and she didn't know what it was. But it inspired a momentary feeling of panic inside her, as if her body sensed a connection she didn't want to feel. She didn't know why she should feel that way. His appearance was unexpected, that was true, but could that be responsible for her sudden unease? She decided rather tensely that it must be his resemblance to Andrew that was upsetting her.

Yet she sensed it was more than that. They were both tall

men, with dark hair and the olive skin of their Mediterranean forebears, but she could hardly compare this man's haggard looks with his son's handsome features. Besides, Gabriel Webb's face had a much harsher cast than Andrew's; less conventionally handsome, she conceded, even without the obvious aftermath of some shock—illness?—she didn't know what. But compelling, even so.

'It was good meeting you at last,' he remarked now, but although Rachel managed a polite acknowledgement she doubted Gabriel Webb's sincerity. He could have no positive thoughts about a woman whom he and the rest of his family had obviously never desired to meet.

He left then, flicking up the collar of his overcoat as he stepped out into the crisp spring air. April had been unseasonably cold, but Rachel wouldn't have thought an overcoat was necessary. Almost irresistibly, she stepped closer to the window, drawing the Roman blind aside to watch him stride away along the street. It had been a disturbing encounter and she wished she didn't have to go back and face Stephanie's grilling. Her friend was bound to want to know chapter and verse and she wondered why she felt so reluctant to discuss him with anyone else.

'Some man, huh?' Stephanie's sardonic voice in her ear made her realise her unguarded interest had not gone unnoticed. 'What did he say?' the other woman added. 'You seemed to be having a pretty intense exchange.'

'That's not true.' Rachel was aware that she had no excuse for her flushed cheeks this time. And, despite her misgivings, she gave in to her own curiosity, 'Do you think he looked all right?'

Stephanie arched inquisitive brows as they walked back to the serving area. 'Is that a serious question?' she asked drily. 'Yeah, I think he looks all right. As all right as any man with a bank account that runs into millions can look, I guess.'

Rachel gave a frustrated sigh. 'That's not what I meant.' She glanced back over her shoulder. 'I just thought he looked as if he'd been ill, that's all. He was very pale, and he had these deep grooves in his cheeks.'

'My heart bleeds,' exclaimed Stephanie unfeelingly. 'For goodness' sake, Rach, you sound as if you feel sorry for him. If he's looking under the weather, it's probably because he's had a heavy night. Men like him are always having heavy nights. That's what they do.'

'You don't know what they do,' retorted Rachel shortly, and was glad when several customers chose that moment to come into the café. It gave her the excuse to end the conversation and attend to them, and she hoped that by the time the midday rush was over Stephanie would have forgotten all about Gabriel Webb and Rachel's ill-advised interest in him.

Rachel's mother brought Hannah into the café as they were closing. She sometimes waited until her granddaughter got home from her school to do her shopping, and then she and Hannah usually called in Rachel's Pantry for a pot of tea and a cream cake, if there were any left.

Rachel was pleased to see them. Although Stephanie hadn't said any more about Gabriel Webb, there had been a certain tension between them all afternoon and Rachel was relieved to find that it was almost five o'clock. The small café, which opened at eight-thirty most mornings, closed at five, and she wouldn't be sorry to get home tonight.

'Hello, sweetheart,' she said, bending to give her small daughter a hug, and Hannah's pale cheeks filled with becoming colour.

''Lo, Mummy,' she answered, clinging to her mother's arm when she would have drawn away. 'May I have a Coke today, please? Please?'

'I'll think about it,' said Rachel lightly, taking charge of her daughter's wheelchair and fitting the wheels under the edge of the nearest table. 'How about you, Mum? Tea, as usual?'

'That would be wonderful,' agreed Mrs Redfern, subsiding into the chair beside her granddaughter. Then, with her usual perception, 'Is anything wrong?'

'No.' Rachel's response was rather too hasty. 'What could be wrong?' she added, heading towards the counter. 'One Coke and one tea coming up.'

'I'll get them,' said Stephanie, meeting her as she rounded the end of the counter, and Rachel met her diffident gaze with some relief.

'Oh, would you?'

'Hey, I'd do anything for my favourite girl,' Stephanie exclaimed more confidently, exchanging a wave with Hannah. 'Hi there, honeybun. Have you had a good day at school?'

'I got a gold star,' Hannah called back proudly. 'Do you want to see it?'

'Can I?' Stephanie made the tea and set two cups on the tray. Then, flicking the cap on a bottle of Coke, she carried the order to the table. 'My, aren't you the clever girl?' she went on, admiring the stick-on gold star Hannah was exhibiting on the lapel of her blazer. 'What was this for? Talking in class?'

'No, silly.' Hannah giggled, and, dropping into the spare chair at the table, Rachel was grateful to her friend for not allowing their differences to interfere with the attention she always showed towards her daughter. 'We did some spellings and I got all mine right.' She beamed at her mother. 'Twenty out of twenty!'

'Goodness!' Rachel pretended to be amazed. 'Well, I think that deserves a special treat. What would you say to a banana split? I think I've got some ice cream left in the freezer.'

'Ooh, yes.' Hannah loved banana splits. 'And can I have some of those sprinkly bits on it, too?'

After Hannah was served, and Mrs Redfern had accepted a vanilla slice, Stephanie said her goodbyes and left them to it. Rachel turned the sign on the door to 'Closed', dropped the blinds, and then came back to her chair.

'You look tired,' said her mother consideringly. 'You're working too hard, Rachel. You really should take a day off now and then.'

'I take every Sunday off,' replied Rachel, sipping her tea. She smiled at Hannah before adding, 'Remind me, I need to speak to Joe Collins before the weekend. That second oven isn't working properly, but I'm hoping we can manage until Sunday.'

Her mother nodded. 'He'll probably say you need a new one. This isn't the first time it's let you down.'

'If it can be repaired, he'll repair it,' declared Rachel firmly. She watched her daughter for a moment. 'I can see you're enjoying that.' There was ice cream smeared all over the little girl's mouth.

'Hmm.'

Hannah was too intent on the sundae to offer more than a mumbled response, and, taking the opportunity to speak to her daughter uninterrupted, Mrs Redfern murmured, 'Have you and Stephanie been having words? You could have cut the atmosphere between you two with a knife when I came in.'

'Oh, don't say that.' Rachel groaned. 'People come in here to relax, not to be greeted by a wave of hostility.'

'So you and Stephanie *have* had words.' Mrs Redfern grimaced. 'Well, you needn't worry. I doubt anyone else would have noticed. It's just that I know you so well. What happened? Was she late again?'

'Well, she was, but that didn't matter.'

'So? Rachel?'

'Oh, if you must know, Gabriel Webb came in this morning.'

'Gabriel Webb?' Mrs Redfern was taken aback. 'Andrew's father?'

Rachel's mouth compressed. 'Do you know any other Gabriel Webbs?'

Her mother shook her head. 'What did he want?'

Rachel sighed and gave Mrs Redfern an old-fashioned look. 'What do people usually want when they come into a café? He wanted a pot of tea. What else?'

Her mother looked nonplussed. 'I wouldn't have thought this was the kind of place someone like Gabriel Webb would frequent.'

'No.' Rachel spoke resignedly. 'You're the second person who's said that today.'

'Stephanie,' guessed Mrs Redfern shrewdly. 'Is that what you fell out about?'

'No.'

'Well, I hope you let him see what you thought of him and his family.'

'Mum!' Rachel stared at her. 'This is a café. Where would I be if I adopted that kind of attitude with my customers?'

'Not all customers,' retorted her mother shortly. 'Just those you don't like.'

Rachel shook her head. 'I can't do that.'

'Of course you can. Isn't there some law about the management of an establishment reserving the right to refuse to serve unwelcome visitors?'

'This is a café, Mum, not a public house.' Rachel picked up a paper napkin and wiped her daughter's chin before adding, 'In any case, I had no reason to say anything. He was served—Patsy served him, not me—he drank his tea, paid his bill and left. End of story.'

'Then why did you and Stephanie fall out?' asked Mrs Redfern irritably. 'I bet she doesn't approve of him coming here.'

'Who are you talking about?' asked Hannah suddenly, belatedly realising she might be missing out on something here, and Rachel gave her mother an impatient look.

'No one you know, sweetheart,' she assured the little girl

firmly. Then, 'And I don't care whether Stephanie approves of him or not.'

'Ah.' Mrs Redfern sniffed. 'I knew he'd have something to do with it. Honestly, Rachel, you haven't seen any of the Webbs for years, but no sooner do you get involved with them than they're creating trouble.'

'That's ridiculous!' Rachel didn't honestly know why she felt the need to defend Gabriel Webb, but she did. 'If you must know, Stephanie annoyed me because she made a comment about his appearance.' She sighed, and then went on stolidly, 'The man looked ill, Mum. And I don't think a few late nights would do it.'

Her mother looked offended now. 'I wouldn't have thought you'd care, one way or the other.'

'Did I say I cared?' Rachel was growing weary of this exchange. 'For heaven's sake, you're worse than Steph. The man's entitled to take a break when he feels like it, and if he chooses to come in here for it, who am I to object?'

'Well, I never thought I'd live to hear you defending one of the Webbs,' replied Mrs Redfern tersely. 'I'd heard he'd come back to live at Copleys, but I would have hoped you'd have more sense than to have anything to do with him.'

Rachel gasped. 'I haven't had anything to do with him,' she protested. 'I hadn't even spoken to him before today. In any case, my quarrel wasn't with him. It was with Andrew. And you're right; I never want to see *him* again.'

'Andrew only did what his father told him,' retorted her mother impatiently. 'I just wish I knew why the man's suddenly decided to grace Kingsbridge with his presence again. The last I heard, he was spending some time in Italy. He should have stayed there.'

Rachel didn't say anything. If Gabriel Webb had been staying in Italy recently, it certainly wasn't evident from his appearance. Far more likely that he'd been staying at the apartment he owned in London. But she doubted that would account for the pallor in his face.

Although the original laboratory had been built at Kingsbridge, there were branches of Webb's Pharmaceuticals all over the continent now, but the head office was still in London. She knew because Andrew had told her, and, knowing also what Andrew had said about how hard his father worked, it seemed much more probable that his strained look was due to exhaustion and not, as Stephanie had implied, from burning the candle at both ends.

Whatever, she was more than content to change the subject, and when Hannah distracted her attention by proudly displaying her empty dish, Rachel hoped that, like her, her mother would consider the subject closed.

CHAPTER TWO

THERE were a couple of occasions during the remainder of that week, when customers came into the café, that Rachel's eyes were drawn to the door. Particularly if a man entered alone. But, although once she had thought it was him, her apprehensions were not realised. Gabriel Webb didn't come back and she told herself it was just as well.

On Sunday morning Joe Collins, who ran his own small electrical business, arrived to take a look at the faulty cooker. A divorcee, in his late thirties, Joe had expended considerable time and energy over the years trying to persuade Rachel to go out with him. But although he was kind and good-looking—and extremely good with Hannah—Rachel had no desire to get involved with anyone else. Her experience with Andrew Webb had made her wary and, despite her mother's assertion that she'd never find anyone more suitable than Joe, she continued to turn down his invitations.

And, as Mrs Redfern had surmised, he considered that Rachel ought to think about replacing the oven. 'The trouble is, it's not easy to get the spares for these old machines,' he declared, after making a temporary repair. 'It's okay for the time being, but I can't guarantee how long it'll last.'

Rachel sighed. 'Well, I can't think about getting a new oven at the moment,' she confessed, as she made them both an espresso coffee. 'They cost the earth, as you know, and I'm going to have to wait until my overdraft is a little more healthy before asking Mr Lawrence for another advance.'

'Well, I might be able to get you a second-hand one,' offered Joe, propping his hips against the counter and spooning two sugars into his coffee. 'You've probably heard that Chadwick's bakery is closing? Yeah? So, I've been offered

17

the job of stripping out the old ovens. I'd make sure you got a good one. And I'd give it a full service before installing it here.'

Rachel gave him a rueful smile. 'That's really kind of you, Joe, but even a second-hand one is beyond my means at the moment. Maybe in six months' time…'

Joe's fair skin reddened. 'You wouldn't have to pay me straight away, Rach. We could say you'd taken it on approval and go on from there.'

'I don't think so.' Rachel knew exactly what he was saying and she couldn't agree to it. 'Besides, if you pulled the old oven out, goodness knows what else might need doing. Those tiles above it are bound to need renewing, and then we'd need a whole new paint job. No, for the present I'm just going to have to make do. But thanks for the offer. I appreciate it.'

'Do you?' Joe regarded her without conviction. 'I thought we were friends, Rach. Friends do stuff for one another. They don't always have to have a reason for offering their help.'

'I know.' Rachel felt uncomfortable now. It wasn't often that Joe stood his ground, and she didn't want to hurt his feelings. 'Well—I'll think about it.' She picked up her coffee and sipped the steaming liquid. Then, seeking an outlet, she added, 'How's your mother?'

'She's fine.' Joe appeared to accept the diversion. 'How's yours? And Hannah, of course.'

'Oh—they're okay, thanks.' Rachel relaxed a little. 'Hannah's doing really well at school. She got a gold star earlier in the week.'

'Clever Hannah.' Joe grinned. 'She's a good kid. Larry would have been proud of her.'

'Yes.'

Rachel didn't argue, but privately she wondered. Larry had never wanted children, despite what he'd said to other people, and Rachel sometimes wondered how he'd have reacted to his daughter's disability if he'd lived.

'I suppose you've heard that Gabe Webb is living at Copleys again,' Joe said suddenly, and Rachel wondered which was worse: talking about her late husband or discussing the man who had been in her thoughts far too often during the past week.

'Um—yes, I knew,' she answered, disappearing into the kitchen to rinse her cup at the sink. She hesitated, and then called back, 'Do you know why?'

Joe came to the kitchen door, watching her as she worked. 'I've heard he's been advised to take things easy for a while,' he said, handing over his cup when she reached for it. 'Andrew's not with him. Well, not as far as I know.'

'Do you think I care where Andrew Webb is?'

'I thought you might.'

'Well, you're wrong.' Rachel was surprised to find she meant it. 'After the way he behaved—' She broke off, realising she'd said too much, and continued less emotively, 'Anyway, it was all a long time ago now. I've moved on.'

'Have you?' Joe's mouth twisted and there was scepticism in his tone. 'I don't see you letting any other man into your life.'

'I don't need a man in my life,' retorted Rachel shortly. 'I don't want one.' She coloured. 'I'm sorry if you think that sounds arrogant. It's just the way I feel.'

Joe's mouth compressed. 'Are you still in love with Larry?'

'No!' Rachel knew she sounded too vehement, but she couldn't help it. She doubted she'd ever been in love with Larry Kershaw. She'd thought she was when they got married, but she'd soon found out that Larry's prime concern was for himself and it was still hard for her to forgive him for causing the accident that had paralysed their daughter. 'I don't think I believe in love any more.'

Joe shook his head. 'Oh, Rachel!' he exclaimed. 'I know you've had a rough time with both Larry and Andrew, but there are men, like myself, who don't consider the world owes them anything. I care about you; you know that. You and Hannah. And I would do my best to make you happy.'

'I know you would.' Rachel felt awful now. She'd never wanted this to happen. 'I just don't think you should waste your time with me.'

'It wouldn't be a waste of time.'

'It would.' Rachel was adamant. 'Believe me.' She put the teatowel aside and squared her shoulders. 'How much do I owe you?'

The following week was busy. The weather was warmer and Kingsbridge's proximity to both Cheltenham and Oxford meant it got quite a few tourists in the season. The ruined priory at Black Ford and the Norman church of St Agnes attracted visitors, and Rachel's Pantry benefited from the increased traffic.

Thankfully, Stephanie hadn't referred to Gabriel Webb again, and Rachel was grateful. In her opinion, far too much had been said about him already, and she was more than willing to put the man out of her mind.

Then, on Wednesday morning, he returned. He came into the café at about half-past ten, and seated himself at the same table in the window. He didn't look in Rachel's direction, but she was perfectly sure her presence had not gone unnoticed and her stomach tightened in unwelcome anticipation.

As luck would have it, she'd just sent Patsy to the bank for some change, so unless she asked Stephanie to serve him she would have to do it, and she wondered a little uncharitably whether he had deliberately chosen that moment to make his entrance. But that would imply that he'd been watching the café and, realising she was being paranoid, Rachel picked up her order pad and crossed the room.

'Can I help you?'

Gabriel Webb looked up at her with dark enigmatic eyes. He looked no less haggard today than he had done on that other occasion, and she wondered how she could still find him attractive when he had obviously made no effort to shave that morning. A dark layer of stubble shadowed his jawline and the collar of his black overcoat enhanced the olive cast of his skin.

'Yes,' he said, after a moment's disturbing appraisal of her face. 'I'd like a pot of tea, please.'

Rachel made a point of writing his order down. Anything to avoid the piercing scrutiny of his dark eyes. 'Anything else?'

His hesitation was deliberate, she was sure. 'What would you suggest?'

Rachel moistened her dry lips. 'Oh—I don't know. A cream cake? A doughnut? A scone?'

Gabriel Webb's lean mouth took on a sardonic curve. 'Thank you, but I don't think so.' He paused. 'I don't suppose you'd care to join me?'

'Me?' Rachel almost squeaked the word. Then, clearing her throat, 'I'm afraid I can't. I—I have work to do.'

Gabriel Webb inclined his head. 'Of course. I shouldn't have suggested it. I'm sorry.'

So was she, but Rachel squashed the treacherous thought. Instead, she allowed a faint smile to indicate her approval and hurried away to get his tea. But her hands shook as she added milk and sugar to the tray she was preparing and Stephanie, who had been loading the dishwasher in the other room, noticed her agitation.

'What's the mat—? Oh, it's him again!'

Stephanie had noticed the new arrival and the censure in her voice was unmistakable. But Rachel was determined not to get into another argument over Gabriel Webb. 'Would you like to deliver his order?' she asked, putting the teapot on the tray, trying to keep her voice expressionless, and her friend gave her an old-fashioned look.

'Why me?' she asked. 'It's obviously you he wants to see. I wonder why?'

Rachel stifled a groan. 'Steph! Don't start that again. Okay. I'll take it to him myself.'

Somehow, she managed to deliver the tray without any mishaps, but when she would have turned away again Gabriel Webb's voice stopped her. 'How are you?' he asked. 'How's that little girl of yours? Hannah, isn't it?'

Rachel's jaw dropped. 'How do you know I have a little girl?' she demanded, her voice rising slightly before she determinedly controlled it. 'Oh, I suppose Andrew told you.'

'He did, actually. But I already knew,' replied Gabriel Webb evenly. 'I have—employees—who make it their business to keep me informed about the women my son goes out with.'

Rachel's face flamed. 'Spies, you mean?' She was furious with him for embarrassing her like this. 'If you'll excuse me, Mr Webb, I have work—'

'You didn't answer my question.'

'And I don't intend to.' Rachel wanted to rush away, but she determinedly stood her ground. 'Don't insult me by pretending that either you or your son care about me or my affairs. You didn't approve of me a year ago, and I doubt very much that you approve of me now.'

Gabriel Webb's mouth tightened. 'I don't recall having an opinion either way a year ago,' he told her steadily. 'And I can't speak for Andrew, of course, but my enquiry was sincere. I only recently discovered why your relationship with my son ended. I was—*I am*—appalled at his behaviour.'

Rachel's expression was scornful. 'Do you really expect me to believe that you didn't know what he thought about Hannah?' she demanded. 'When you freely admit that you keep tabs on the women in his life?'

'Believe it or not, no one saw the need to inform me that the child was disabled,' he replied, his dark eyes intent and compelling. 'After all, the affair with Andrew was soon over.' His lips twisted. 'As his affairs usually are, I have to admit.'

Rachel held up her head. 'Hannah isn't disabled,' she declared stiffly. 'She's a perfectly normal little girl who happens to be—temporarily—confined to a wheelchair.'

'Temporarily?'

'We believe so, yes,' insisted Rachel, crossing her fingers behind her back. 'Her doctor seems to think there's nothing physically wrong with her. She just doesn't—want to walk.'

Or get into a car with a man, or talk about the accident, Rachel added to herself. But that was no concern of his.

Gabriel frowned. 'Who gave you that prognosis?'

'Does it matter?' Rachel disliked the knowledge that she wanted to confide in him. 'Now, I really must get on...'

'Of course.'

This time he accepted her assertion and Rachel turned quickly away. For a moment she'd half expected him to argue with her, and as she made her way back to the service area she realised with a pang that she had not only said more than she'd intended, but she was sorry their conversation was over.

'Well, that looked fairly painless,' remarked Stephanie drily when Rachel returned to installing plastic-wrapped packs of sandwiches into the refrigerated display. 'I gather the two of you found you had something in common, after all. Let me guess: Andrew!'

'You're wrong.' Rachel gave her friend a defensive stare. 'He was asking about Hannah, if you must know.'

'Hannah?' Stephanie was surprised. 'How does he know about Hannah?'

'How do you think?' Rachel refused to tell Stephanie that Gabriel Webb had had her investigated. In fact, the more she thought about that aspect of the situation the less she liked it, and she chided herself for allowing him to manipulate her as he had. Unknowingly, her fingers crushed the egg and mayo sandwich she was holding. 'Dammit, how much longer is Patsy going to be?'

'Too long to stop you from mangling that sandwich anyway,' observed Stephanie, taking the plastic container from her. 'Don't worry, I'm not going to say anything. The way you choose to deal with your affairs is nothing to do with me.'

Rachel's shoulders sagged. 'I'm sorry, Steph. I'm being bitchy again, aren't I?' She grimaced. 'It's that man! He brings out the worst in me. If he comes in here again, you'll have to serve him. Or Patsy. If she ever gets back from the bank.'

Stephanie pulled a wry face. 'He hasn't left yet,' she pointed out ruefully. 'And, judging by the way he was watching you as you walked back here, he'll be back.'

Rachel made sure she was in the kitchen when Gabriel came to pay his bill. But although she assured herself that she didn't care what he said, she found herself straining to hear his exchange with Patsy, and her nerves tightened when she heard the younger girl laugh at something he said.

Which was ridiculous, she knew, but that didn't make a blind bit of difference to the way she felt. Somehow, some way, Gabriel Webb had got under her skin, and if she was totally honest with herself she'd admit that she'd found challenging him an exhilarating experience.

After what Stephanie had said, Rachel half expected Gabriel to return to the café the next morning. But he didn't. An overcast sky heralded a change in the weather, and by late afternoon it was raining quite heavily. Rachel was relieved when her mother and Hannah came into the café at a quarter to five, shaking the dampness from their umbrella. It signified that the working day was almost over.

'I want a banana split,' announced Hannah, almost as soon as her grandmother had pushed her though the door, and although there were few patrons still left in the café, Rachel gave her a reproving stare.

'I want never gets,' she said, quoting one of her mother's

favourite sayings. Then, transferring her attention to the older woman, she asked, 'How did she behave today?'

'I was good, I was good,' cried Hannah, but her mother waited for Mrs Redfern to confirm that the weekly visit to the physiotherapist had been a success.

'She—worked quite hard,' admitted the child's grand-mother dubiously. And then, in an aside to her daughter, 'I just wish we didn't have to deal with that woman. She's so—unsympathetic. I sometimes think Hannah would do much better with someone else.'

Rachel sighed. She'd heard this complaint before. 'What can we do?' she asked. 'Dr Williams arranged for Hannah to see her. And Mrs Stone is supposed to be one of the best physiotherapists around.'

'Who said that?' Mrs Redfern wasn't convinced. 'Stone by name and Stone by nature, if you ask me. Not to mention the fact that she makes me feel like I'm an unnecessary en-cumbrance.'

'Oh, Mum, you're exaggerating!'

'What is Grandma 'xaggerating?' asked Hannah, getting impatient. Then tugging on her mother's skirt, she pleaded, 'Can I have a banana split, please? Can I? I promise I'll eat all my supper.'

'May I?' corrected Rachel automatically. 'I don't know how many times I've told you that.' She sighed again. 'Oh, I suppose so. But I'll have to get it myself. Steph's already gone home.'

'So early?' murmured Mrs Redfern, waiting until the last two customers had left the café before wheeling Hannah's chair across to the counter.

'She had some shopping to do,' said Rachel levelly, not rising to the bait. Her mother considered that Stephanie didn't pull her weight in the café. And it was true that the other woman was inclined to take advantage of the fact that she and Rachel were friends.

'Shopping!' Mrs Redfern snorted, but, seeing that her

daughter was not in the mood to bite, she changed the subject to one Rachel liked even less. 'By the way, you'll never guess what I heard this morning: there's a rumour that the reason Gabriel Webb is living at Copleys now is because he's seeing a consultant neurologist at a hospital in Oxford.'

Rachel was stunned at her reaction to this news. Anxiety blossomed in her stomach, and she didn't know how she controlled the urge to demand that her mother tell her where she had heard such a thing. God, she thought, turning away to take the ice cream out of the freezer, giving herself time to recover. Was that why he looked so pale and drawn? Because he was ill? Dear Lord, what was wrong with him?

'Can I have some of the fluffy cream that comes out of a can as well?' Hannah's request was sobering. She had wheeled herself round to the other side of the counter and had dipped her finger into the sauce her mother had poured over the fruit. 'Ooh, that's lovely, Mummy. You make the bestest banana split ever!'

'You'd better not let Stephanie hear you say that,' said Rachel, forcing herself to put her concerns about Gabriel Webb to the back of her mind. But she was aware that her voice wasn't quite as playful as it should have been and she felt her mother watching her with shrewd eyes.

'I always like the things you do best,' declared Hannah staunchly, clearly sensing that she was on to a winner. 'Do you think I could have a milkshake as well?'

Rachel pulled a wry face. 'Don't push it, sweetheart,' she advised, handing the dish containing the banana split to her mother and guiding Hannah's chair to the nearest table. 'There we are.' This as Mrs Redfern set the dish down in front of her granddaughter. 'Now I'll go and make us a nice cup of tea.'

'All right.'

Hannah accepted her mother's decision good-naturedly, and Rachel was leaning down to give the little girl a swift hug when the café door opened behind her.

A draught of damp air issued into the room, but it wasn't the sudden drop in temperature that caused Rachel to straighten and glance round in wary understanding. It was her mother's sharp intake of breath and the shocked expression that had crossed her face.

'Am I intruding?'

Gabriel Webb stood just inside the door, his dark hair sparkling with drops of rain, the familiar overcoat hanging open over black jeans and a V-necked cream sweater. Ironically enough, he looked less drawn today, his eyes surveying the scene he had interrupted with narrow-eyed consideration.

'Oh, Mr Webb.' Rachel was aware of feeling totally out of her depth. Aware, too, that her mother was watching her reaction closely and probably not liking what she saw. 'I— I'm sorry but we're closed.'

Gabriel turned and flicked the card that still displayed the 'Open' sign. 'Is that right?' he murmured. 'I didn't realise. When I saw you still had customers...'

Rachel couldn't look at her mother. She was fairly sure Gabriel Webb knew exactly who her 'customers' were, and she could sense Mrs Redfern's antagonism from across the table. But, short of calling him a liar, she had no choice but to introduce them.

'Um—this is my mother and my daughter, Mr Webb,' she said awkwardly. Then, with a hopeful glance in her mother's direction, 'Mum, this is Mr Webb.' She hesitated a moment before adding reluctantly, 'Andrew's father.'

Mrs Redfern didn't get up. 'Yes, I know who Mr Webb is, Rachel,' she declared stiffly, without offering him a greeting. 'Hannah, watch what you're doing. You're dripping ice cream all over the table.'

'Who's Mr Webb?' Hannah hissed to her grandmother in the kind of stage whisper that had to be audible to their visitor, and Rachel stifled a groan.

'Hannah!' she reproved, before Mrs Redfern could say anything more provocative, and then caught her breath when

Gabriel left his position by the door to approach the table where the older woman and the child were sitting.

'Hi, Hannah,' he said, squatting down beside her chair and regarding her with warm approving eyes. 'That looks good.'

Hannah cast a nervous glance up at her mother and then, apparently deciding there was no harm in answering him, she said, 'It's a banana split.'

'Yeah, I know what it is.' Gabriel grinned, and Rachel realised it was the first time she had seen him so relaxed. 'I used to love them when I was younger. Banana splits and strawberry milkshakes! I think those were my favourite things.'

'Do you like strawberry milkshakes, too?' asked Hannah, wide-eyed. 'They're my very favourite drinks. Only Mummy says that having a milkshake as well as a banana split will spoil my supper.'

'Well, I guess Mummy knows best—'

'Eat your ice cream, Hannah.' Mrs Redfern had evidently had enough of this interruption to their routine. She looked at Gabriel. 'I'm sure you've got better things to do than waste time talking to a six-year-old, Mr Webb. As Rachel told you, the café's closed. It was my fault. I forgot to lock the door.'

Gabriel got to his feet. 'No problem,' he said easily, his eyes moving from the older woman's tight closed face to Rachel's embarrassed one. 'You've got a very pretty daughter, Rachel,' he appended. 'I envy you.'

Rachel's lips parted. She didn't know what to say. Or, at least, she knew what she ought to say, what her mother was expecting her to say, but she couldn't do it.

'Thank you,' she murmured instead, conscious of him in a way that was totally personal, totally inappropriate. 'I'm sorry about—about the sign.'

'Yeah.'

He held her gaze for a moment longer than was necessary and Rachel felt as if the world around her had shifted on its axis. Then, with a murmured word of farewell for Hannah and a polite nod in Mrs Redfern's direction, he started towards the door.

Rachel hesitated only briefly before going after him. She had to lock the door, she defended herself, but she could tell from her mother's expression that she wasn't deceived. Mrs Redfern looked as if she knew exactly what her daughter was thinking, and Rachel wished she wasn't so transparent.

It was still raining, heavily, and Gabriel halted in the doorway. 'Do you have transport?' he asked, his eyes on her averted face, and Rachel quickly nodded.

'Oh, yes,' she assured him, wondering what he would have done if she'd said no. 'Um—do you?'

It was a stupid question and she knew it. The Webbs owned a fleet of cars. They employed a chauffeur, for heaven's sake. He would think she was a complete idiot for asking.

But instead of answering her, he asked her a question. 'What would you do if I said no?'

Rachel's breath caught in her throat. 'I don't know.' She moistened her lips. 'Offer to call you a taxi, I suppose.'

'Ah.' His mouth took on a sardonic curve. 'I imagine it would be awkward if you suggested anything else.'

Rachel's hand sought an unruly strand of her honey-streaked brown hair and tucked it behind her ear. Then, 'Like what?' she asked rather breathlessly, and he smiled.

'Well, it's obvious I'd not be your mother's favourite choice of travelling companion,' he remarked drily. 'That is, if you were thinking of offering me a lift home.' He paused. 'Which, of course, you're not.'

Rachel straightened her spine. 'I think you're teasing me, Mr Webb. I'm sorry you've had a wasted journey—'

'It wasn't a wasted journey,' he contradicted her softly. 'It gave me the opportunity to meet your charming little daughter.'

'And why would you want to meet Han—my daughter?' asked Rachel tensely, aware that her mother was getting more and more irritated with this exchange. With good reason, she acknowledged wryly. She should have avoided any attempt to prolong this conversation.

'I didn't say it was my prime objective,' he retorted now, turning up his collar against the rain and contemplating the weather with resignation. 'Meeting Hannah was a bonus.'

Rachel stared at him then. In profile, his face had a harsh beauty despite its strength. Narrow cheekbones hollowed beneath heavy lids and his lean mouth had a sensual appeal. His appearance disturbed her and she knew again that unwelcome twinge of panic at the realisation. She didn't want to feel the emotions he aroused inside her.

'I think you'd better go, Mr Webb,' she said stiffly, scared she might betray herself in some way, and flinched when he turned his narrow-eyed gaze upon her.

'Call me Gabriel—or Gabe, if you'd prefer it,' he said, his eyes on her mouth. Then, before she could object, he added, 'There's my car,' and strode purposefully across the street to get into the back of a silver-grey Mercedes that had been idling in the 'No Parking' area. He raised his hand as the car drove away but Rachel didn't respond. She was still trying to come to terms with the fact that it was she he had wanted to see.

CHAPTER THREE

'HAVE you seen that man again?'

It was Sunday evening and Rachel was in the process of bathing her daughter. Hannah loved being in the tub, and although Rachel knew it was wishful thinking, she sometimes thought the little girl actually moved her legs in the soapy water.

Mrs Redfern had come to stand in the bathroom doorway and Rachel glanced briefly over her shoulder. She and her mother and Hannah shared this house in Maple Avenue, which had been the Redferns' family home for the past twenty-five years. Her father had died over ten years ago, and when Larry had been killed in the car accident that had paralysed their daughter it had seemed sensible for Rachel to move back in with her mother. The house was big enough to accommodate a family, goodness knew, and Rachel had never regretted her decision.

Without her mother to look after Hannah she could never have returned to college or gone into business for herself. She wouldn't have had the security she enjoyed now without the older woman's help, and she felt instantly guilty for the resentment that swelled inside her at her mother's words. Mrs Redfern had said little about Gabriel Webb since she'd offered her opinion of his character after he'd left the café on that Thursday afternoon, but Rachel realised she had been waiting for her to refer to him again.

'What man?' asked Hannah at once, ever alert to any gossip, and Rachel gave her mother a telling look.

'No one you know,' she said shortly, justifying the lie to herself. Then, with another warning glance in her mother's direction, 'No, I haven't. Have you?'

Mrs Redfern's lips pursed. 'There's no need to take that attitude, Rachel. It was a perfectly reasonable question. But, if you insist on burying your head in the sand—'

'Why would you bury your head in the sand, Mummy?' Hannah was puzzled. 'Does Grandma mean at the seaside?'

'Something like that,' said Rachel shortly, soaping the sponge and applying it rather aggressively to the little girl's shoulders. Hannah protested, and Rachel was instantly contrite. 'I'm sorry, sweetheart,' she exclaimed. 'I wasn't thinking.'

'Well, I think the truth is that you were,' retorted Mrs Redfern tersely, going out of the bathroom and slamming the door behind her, and Rachel expelled a weary breath.

That was all she needed: for her mother to get it into her head that she was interested in Gabriel Webb. It was ridiculous! Ludicrous! He was Andrew's father, for God's sake! He had to be at least twenty years older than she was.

'Is Grandma cross?'

Hannah's anxious question reminded her that she had a sensitive child to deal with, and Rachel quickly rescued her expression. 'Grandma's not cross with you,' she assured the little girl with a bright smile. 'Now, come on. Let me lift you onto the seat and we'll shower you off.'

It was comparatively easy to divert Hannah's attention, but later that evening Rachel was forced to face her mother's censure again. With her daughter safely tucked up in bed there was no third party to provide a distraction, and although Rachel had got out her account books in the hope of avoiding a confrontation she soon found she had wasted her time.

'Stephanie tells me Gabriel Webb has been into the café more than once in the last two weeks,' Mrs Redfern remarked, carrying the cup of coffee she had just made herself into her late husband's study, where Rachel was working. 'That's without that evening he came after the girls had gone home.'

Rachel knew a momentary twinge of anger towards her

friend for relating something so potentially explosive to her
mother, and then chided herself for blaming anyone else for
this situation. 'So?' she said managing to adopt an indifferent
tone. 'I told you he'd been in.'

'Not three times,' retorted Mrs Redfern, taking the chair
across the desk. 'What does he want?'

Rachel was glad the lamplight shone down on the account
books and not on her face. 'Why should he want anything?'
she protested. 'Other than a decent pot of tea, of course. You
won't deny that I serve one of the best cups of tea in the
area?'

'Oh, Rachel!' There was a wealth of impatience in Mrs
Redfern's voice. 'I know you're not as naïve as you'd like
me to think. I saw the way he was looking at you the other
afternoon. I find it hard to believe, I admit, that a man like
him—a man with his money, with his *background*,' she
amended quickly, 'should be interested in someone his
son—'

'Don't,' said Rachel shortly. 'Please don't.'

'Don't what?'

'Don't say anything more,' said Rachel, aware that her
nails were digging into her palms. 'It's not true, so why tor-
ment yourself over it? Gabriel Webb is not interested in me.'

'Then why is he always in the café?'

Rachel gasped. 'He's not *always* in the café,' she exclaimed frustratedly. 'As you said, he's been in three times
in as many weeks. That's hardly a record. I have customers
who come in two or three times a day!'

'Well, according to Steph—'

'Look, I don't care what Steph thinks,' replied Rachel,
wishing her friend would mind her own business. 'Ask yourself the question, Mum. Why would someone like him feel
anything but—but curiosity about me?'

'Curiosity?' Mrs Redfern considered this possibility seriously, and Rachel had the feeling she'd said the wrong thing.
But then, discarding that thought, her mother returned to her

original opinion. 'You're an attractive woman, Rachel. If you had more confidence in yourself you'd see that I was right.'

'Oh, Mum!' Rachel was weary of this conversation. 'I'm too tall, I'm too thin, and I have a hairstyle that was in fashion ten years ago. I'm not beautiful or sexy. I appreciate your loyalty, but I fear it's misplaced.'

'That's the trouble with you,' responded her mother at once. 'Always putting yourself down. You'd never have married Larry Kershaw if you hadn't had such a low opinion—'

'No more, Mum.' Rachel groaned. This was an old argument and one she had no wish to get into tonight. Then, because she had to, 'If I hadn't married Larry I wouldn't have had Hannah. And even you can't deny that she's been a delight ever since she was born.'

'If Larry hadn't spent as much time in the pub, Hannah would still be a normal little girl,' retorted Mrs Redfern tightly. And then, seeing Rachel's shocked face, she hastily recanted. 'I know, I know. Hannah *is* a normal little girl.' She took a sip of her coffee. 'I just wish—I just wish—'

'Don't we all?' said Rachel flatly, determinedly picking up her pen. 'I've got to get on, Mum. I mean it. It's nearly nine o'clock and these accounts won't calculate themselves.'

Monday and Tuesday passed without incident, and Rachel was beginning to think that both her and her mother's fears had been groundless when Gabriel Webb turned up again. He came into the café on Wednesday afternoon, just as she was about to close. Stephanie and Patsy had already gone— thank goodness, thought Rachel fervently—and as it wasn't a day that Hannah and her grandmother were coming to meet her Rachel was on her own when he appeared.

He was wearing dark trousers and a leather blouson jacket this afternoon, and a dark blue tee shirt that highlighted the olive cast of his skin. His face was still drawn but Rachel was uneasily aware of the hard strength in his lean features. It was an awareness that had come to her gradually, but she couldn't deny he possessed a sort of magnetism that no amount of self-denigration on her part could dismiss.

She didn't want to notice these things but she couldn't help it. It was her mother's fault, she thought crossly. And Stephanie's. They had put these thoughts into her head. Yet in her heart of hearts she knew that it wasn't anything either of them had said that had reduced her to this state of nervous apprehension every time he came into the café. And she was very much afraid he knew it, too.

'I understand,' he said, when she recovered herself sufficiently to glance at the clock. 'You're closing.' He paused. 'I hoped you might be.' He pushed his fingers into the waistline pockets of his trousers and she instantly noticed how his thumbs pointed to the taut fabric that shaped his sex. 'I wondered if you'd like to have a drink with me for a change.'

Rachel swallowed, dragging her eyes away from that part of his anatomy and avoiding his disturbing appraisal by straightening a chair at a nearby table. Then, because she had to say something and she couldn't possibly accept his invitation, 'I'm sorry, Mr Webb. I'm just on my way home.'

'My name's Gabe, as I believe I told you,' he said, standing squarely between her and the door. 'And I'm sure you could spare me a few minutes of your valuable time. The Golden Lion's just across the road.'

Rachel shook her head. 'I don't think so.'

'Why not?' His impatience was carefully controlled. 'Have you got another appointment?'

'No.' Rachel sighed. 'I've just told you. I'm on my way home.'

'So why can't you humour me and save me from a lonely half-hour in the pub?'

Rachel caught her lower lip between her teeth. 'I can't believe you have to rely on a perfect stranger for company,' she said, and saw the way his jaw compressed. She was angering him, she could tell that, and she thought perhaps that was the way to go. Whatever impulse had caused this un-

expected petition, it couldn't possibly survive a blank denial.
'I'm sorry.'

'You still haven't given me a convincing reason why not,'
he persisted. Then, harshly, 'Am I trespassing on another
man's property? Is that it?'

Rachel's jaw dropped. 'I just don't want to have a drink
with you, Mr Webb.' She picked up the navy jacket she had
dropped over the back of a chair and pushed her arms into
the sleeves. 'I'm tired and I'm looking forward to having a
long soak in the bath. Does that answer your question?'

Gabriel didn't move. 'You don't like me,' he said flatly.
'I had thought, after our conversation the other afternoon,
that you'd realised that I am not my son.'

'Oh, I do realise that, Mr Webb.' Rachel was getting angry
now. 'But what you don't seem capable of grasping is that I
run a café. I have to be polite to all my customers, even those
I—I—'

'You don't like,' he finished for her drily. 'Yes. I get the
picture.'

Rachel doubted that he did. And there was such a look of
defeat in his night-dark eyes now that she felt dreadful. When
he'd come into the café there'd been a different expression
on his face, but that anticipation—that expectation—had all
been extinguished now. He looked greyer, older, and when
he turned abruptly towards the door she wanted to flay herself
for destroying his mood.

'Wait…'

Without giving herself time to have second thoughts,
Rachel went after him. Her hand reached for his sleeve, but
her fingers brushed his wrist instead, the leather strap of his
wristwatch so much warmer than his chilled skin.

And, instantly, she wanted to take him into her arms. To
hold him and warm his cold flesh with her body that was
suddenly hot and pulsing with life. But of course she didn't.
Instead, her hand fell awkwardly to her side, and when she

met his guarded stare she wondered what in God's name she had been thinking of.

'Yes?' he said, and now it was her turn to face his closed gaze.

'I—perhaps we could have a drink together,' she said with difficulty, and his mouth took on a mocking curve.

'Don't do me any favours, Mrs Kershaw,' he said, his features cold and withdrawn. 'I don't need your pity.'

'It's not—it's not pity,' protested Rachel, wondering somewhat incredulously why she was persisting with this. Why hadn't she let him go when she'd had the chance? 'However, if you've changed your mind...'

'I haven't changed my mind,' he said heavily, his hand resting on the handle of the door. He paused. 'Do you want to follow me over?'

'I—no.' Rachel realised he was giving her one final chance to escape. 'I can come now. Just let me turn off the lights and set the alarm.'

He was waiting outside when she emerged from the café and locked the door. He was standing, staring across the road at the warm brown stone of the Golden Lion's walls, his hands pushed into the pockets of his jacket. It wasn't a cold evening, but there was an errant breeze that whipped tendrils of dark hair across his temple and he lifted his hand and raked long fingers through his hair as she joined him.

They crossed the street in silence and entered the public house beneath the creaking sign of King Richard's lion. A carpeted foyer with swing doors opened into a discreetly lit bar that at this hour of the afternoon was virtually deserted. Only a couple of regulars occupied stools at the counter, discussing racing form with the bartender, and Gabriel indicated that Rachel should find a seat while he got their drinks.

'Just an orange juice for me,' she murmured when he asked what she wanted, and he raised a resigned brow before approaching the bar.

Windows overlooking the street outside were set high in

the walls, giving privacy to anyone seated in the booths below. Rachel chose a corner location, sliding onto the padded banquette with a feeling of mild disbelief. What was she doing here? she wondered. And with Gabriel Webb! Her mother would never believe it.

Or rather she would, Rachel acknowledged, glancing towards the bar to find her companion exchanging a casual greeting with the bartender. Evidently he was not unknown here, and Rachel wondered if anyone had recognised her as well. Oh, God, she should have insisted on them going somewhere where they weren't immediately recognisable.

'One orange juice,' murmured Gabriel, sliding into the booth opposite, and she was glad he hadn't attempted to sit next to her.

Not that he would, she assured herself, once again aware that she was attributing far too much importance to the situation. He had invited her for a drink. So what?

He had got himself a beer and now he raised the bottle to his lips and drank some of the foaming liquid. Unwillingly, her eyes were drawn to the strong column of his throat and the way his muscles moved under his dark skin. Everything he did caused a quiver of awareness deep inside her, and she wondered why he affected her this way. It couldn't only be pity, could it? *No!* Pity had never felt like this.

He lowered the bottle and wiped his mouth with the back of his hand before saying softly, 'What made you change your mind?'

That wasn't easy to answer, particularly after her thoughts of a few moments ago, and she bent her head, seeking inspiration in her glass. The truth was, she didn't know why she had abandoned all her principles and accepted his invitation. It was far too complex for her to understand.

'I—I suppose I was curious,' she said at last, confessing the least of her sins. 'Why did you invite me?'

Gabriel's mouth twisted. 'Why does a man usually ask a

woman to go out with him?' he asked lightly, and Rachel's skin feathered with apprehension.

'You don't mean that,' she said, her fingers nervous on the base of her glass. 'If Andrew put you up to this—'

'I haven't seen Andrew in weeks,' retorted Gabriel harshly. 'He and I have little in common. And why would you assume I must have some ulterior motive for my invitation?' He paused. 'Unless you think I'm too old to enjoy your company.'

Rachel caught her breath. 'Your age has nothing to do with it.' She moistened dry nervous lips. 'I just find it hard to believe that you'd have any interest in me. And I'd rather you didn't insult my intelligence by pretending you were irresistibly attracted to my womanly charms.'

Gabriel gave a small smile. 'You don't have a very high opinion of yourself, do you?'

'So my mother is always telling me,' replied Rachel tightly. 'Shall we talk about you instead? Like why have you come back to Kingsbridge, for example?'

'That's not important.' He cradled his beer between his palms. 'For the moment I'd like to explain why I wanted to see you again. I realise this is an unusual situation, and I understand that you might be suspicious of my motives.'

'I didn't say that—'

'As good as,' he insisted softly. 'After all, my son did a pretty good job of making you despise him, and because my name's the same you probably think I'm just like him.'

'And you're not?' Rachel sounded sceptical.

'You don't believe that?' He shrugged. 'No, why would you? I've done nothing to prove otherwise. Not yet, anyway.' His eyes narrowed on her soft mouth. 'But if you'll let me, I will.'

Rachel shook her head. 'Why would you want to?'

'Because I like what I know of you,' he said steadily. 'Because I admire you. Because I'd like to get to know you better. Does that answer your question?'

It did, but Rachel didn't know if it was what she wanted to hear. Her reaction to Gabriel Webb troubled her, and she had the distinct feeling that he could hurt her far more than his son had ever done.

She had gone out with Andrew for over three months, it was true, but although she'd been distressed when he'd let her down, her feelings of betrayal had had more to do with Hannah than herself. She couldn't believe she'd let a man like him get close to her, and it had been pride as much as anything that had allowed her to let her friends think that Andrew's father had broken them up.

'You can't expect me to believe that you had any of—of this in mind that first time you came into the café,' she said at last, and a shrug of his shoulders conceded the point.

'No, that's right,' he agreed. 'I don't deny it. I had some time to kill, the café was there, and I'll admit to being curious to meet the woman who had made such a lasting impression on my son.'

Rachel's lips twisted. 'Yeah, right.'

'It's true.' Gabriel studied her disbelieving face. 'Andrew doesn't usually remember his conquests, but you evidently had quite an effect on him.'

'Hannah did, you mean,' said Rachel tersely. 'I'm surprised he told you about her. I wouldn't have thought it was something he'd want to brag about.'

'Did I say he bragged about it?' Gabriel sighed. 'It wasn't like that.'

'And he suddenly told you this, out of the blue, just a few weeks ago?' Rachel sat back in her seat. 'Why would he?'

'Because I'd told him I was coming back to Kingsbridge,' said Gabriel heavily. 'If you must know, he was drunk at the time, or I doubt he'd have said anything.'

'That figures.' Rachel was sardonic. 'So that's why you came into the café: to find out if he'd been telling the truth.'

'That was not why I came into the café,' insisted Gabriel. 'All right; I've told you I was curious to meet you. But, believe me, I felt nothing but disgust when Andrew told me how he felt about Hannah. Until then I'd had no idea that my son was such a—a—'

'Bigot?' suggested Rachel wryly, but Gabriel only shook his head.

'Such a bastard,' he said forcefully. Then, because this was evidently not the way he wanted the conversation to go, he put his beer aside and regarded her with those disturbing dark eyes. 'I can only apologise for my son and hope that you can forgive his ignorance. As far as I'm concerned, I'd like to put the past behind us.'

'Behind *us*?' Rachel felt slightly incredulous. 'There is no us, Mr Webb.'

'Not yet.'

'Not ever,' she declared unsteadily, suddenly in a panic to get out of there. 'I have to go,' she added, sliding to the end of the booth. 'Thank you for the drink—'

'Rachel!' Before she could get to her feet, lean brown fingers closed about her wrist. 'Please. Hear me out.'

'I can't.' Her agitation was too great to allow her to accept his request. 'I'm sorry. I—my mother will be expecting me. She gets worried if I'm late.'

'I'll take you home,' he said flatly. 'Don't ask me how, but I know your mother uses your car to take Hannah to and from her school. You either walk home or take the bus. Am I right?'

Rachel stared at him. 'You've been following us?'

'Not me, no,' said Gabriel reluctantly, releasing her arm and sagging back in his seat, as if the effort of restraining her had exhausted him. 'Now I suppose you'll accuse me of stalking you?'

Rachel didn't know what to say. The panic that had appeared so abruptly had given way to a curious sense of anticipation, and although she knew she ought to be angry with him, there was something about his sudden capitulation that was oddly appealing.

'Why?' she asked helplessly. 'Why are you doing this?'

'I wish to God I knew,' he said in response, a mocking twist to his mouth. 'Believe me, I'm not in the habit of pursuing my son's ex-girlfriends. And, although I was curious about you, I had no intention of making a nuisance of myself.'

'You haven't...' Rachel spoke impulsively and then wished she hadn't. 'I mean—I didn't say that.'

'But you probably thought it, hmm?'

Rachel shrugged. 'I don't understand what you—what you want of me.'

Gabriel's eyes narrowed. 'Is it so inconceivable that I might find your company enjoyable?'

'Frankly, yes.' Rachel was honest.

'Because you think I'm too old to have a sexual relationship?'

A sexual relationship!

Rachel swallowed, too shocked to offer a rational defence. Falling back on platitudes, she murmured, 'You're not old.'

'I wish I could believe you meant that.' He paused. 'How old are you, Rachel? Twenty-four? Twenty-five? I can give you twenty years at least.'

'I'm twenty-eight,' said Rachel shortly. 'Andrew is three years younger than me.'

'And I'm seventeen years older.' He arched a dark brow. 'Twenty years! Seventeen! It's still an awfully long time, isn't it?'

'Who are you trying to convince?' she asked, forced to argue with him, and then flushed at the familiarity in her tone. 'I'm sorry. But you did ask.'

'Hey, don't apologise.' Gabriel was unconcerned. 'I'm encouraged that you feel able to relax with me.' He lifted his beer to his lips, watching her the whole time. Then, after putting it down again, he added, 'I like it.'

Rachel felt totally out of her depth. 'You know, I really

do have to go,' she said at last, glancing at her watch. 'There's a bus that leaves in exactly five minutes—'

'I've said I'll take you home,' Gabriel reminded her. 'Please. Let me. I want to.'

Rachel's limbs melted. It was all too easy to imagine him using those same words in an entirely different context—an entirely sexual context, she acknowledged unsteadily—and it was incredibly difficult to remember that this man was— *could be*—her enemy.

'It's not necessary,' she began, but he was already out of the booth and offering her his hand to help her to her feet.

'Let me be the judge of that,' he said, the expression in his eyes telling her that he knew exactly why she'd pretended not to see his gesture. 'Shall we go?'

CHAPTER FOUR

AN ENORMOUS bouquet of flowers was delivered to the café the following morning. It contained roses and irises, freesias and carnations, and many other species Rachel couldn't identify. Stephanie thought that some of the more exotic blooms were orchids, but Rachel was simply overwhelmed by the size and beauty of the bouquet.

There was a card attached but, as if he was aware that his gift would be contentious enough, Gabriel had merely signed his initials and left her to explain why he'd sent them.

'You mean, you actually went out with him last night and you weren't going to say anything?' Stephanie asked accusingly, when her friend was obliged to explain that she had seen Gabriel Webb again.

'It wasn't that important,' Rachel protested, cradling the bouquet defensively. 'We had a drink together after I closed the café. That was all.'

'All?' Stephanie shook her head. 'But surely you knew that I'd find out sooner or later? Your mother's bound to mention it.'

'Mum doesn't know,' admitted Rachel reluctantly. 'I—I had him drop me at the end of Maple Avenue.'

Stephanie's jaw dropped. 'Why?'

'Why do you think?' Rachel cast her eyes around, looking for vases in which she could arrange the flowers. 'To avoid another confrontation, of course.' She paused. 'Are you going to tell her?'

'Not if you don't want me to.' Stephanie was indignant.

'You told her how many times Gabriel had come into the café,' Rachel reminded her, and the other woman snorted.

'So it's Gabriel now, is it? And as far as telling your

44

mother about him coming here is concerned, I didn't know it was a secret.'

'It's not.' Rachel shook her head a little guiltily now, aware that she had used Gabriel's name far too easily. Even though she insisted on calling him Mr Webb to his face, it was obvious that deep down she didn't think of him that way and the knowledge was disturbing. She supposed she ought to tell her mother the truth about why she and Andrew had split up, and thus clear Gabriel's name in that respect. But wasn't that admitting that she thought there was something between them? She sighed as she looked at Stephanie. 'I—I don't know what to do about it; why he keeps coming here.'

Stephanie gave her a disbelieving look. 'Why do you think?'

'I don't know what to think.'

'Oh, come on, Rachel, you're not that naïve.' Her friend was impatient now. 'He's obviously attracted to you. Don't look at me like that. What other reason could there be?'

Rachel turned away, unwilling to pursue that any further, and, glancing up at the shelves, she said tersely, 'Um—where did we put those vases we used at Christmas?'

'Don't ask me.' Stephanie was equally terse in her response. 'Why don't you send the flowers to a hospital instead? That way you'll not have to worry about your mother asking where they came from.'

'Oh, God!' Rachel groaned. 'I hadn't thought of that.' She looked regretfully down at the flowers in her arms. 'Do you think I should?'

'I think you should do what you want to do,' declared Stephanie, her tone gentling. 'Rach, there's no law that says you shouldn't go out with Gabriel Webb if you want to. He's free and so are you. Okay, so he's probably old enough to be your father. So what? It's nothing to stress about.'

'He's seventeen years older than I am,' said Rachel quietly, and Stephanie arched a speculative brow.

'So you got around to ages, did you? Not such a casual conversation, after all.'

'Stop it.' Rachel sighed. 'Oh, Steph, do you think he feels—well, sorry for me?'

'Sorry for you?' Stephanie blinked. 'Why should he feel sorry for you?'

'I don't know.' Rachel shifted a little awkwardly. 'I suppose because he's used to dealing with much more glamorous women than me.'

'Stop fishing.' Stephanie laughed. 'You know as well as I do that you're just as good-looking now as you were when you married Larry.'

'Which isn't saying much.'

'It's saying a lot.' Stephanie was adamant. 'You're an attractive woman, Rach. Blonde hair—'

'Light brown hair.'

'—green eyes—'

'Hazel.'

'—and slim.' Stephanie patted her own generous hips with a resigned hand. 'Mike calls these my love-handles, but I bet he wishes I looked more like you.'

'That's not true.' Rachel pulled a face. 'Mike thinks the world of you and you know it.' She pulled a crystal container down from the top shelf and put the flowers on the counter. 'Anyway, when are you going to let him make an honest woman of you? It must be six months since you told me he'd asked you to marry him.'

'We're okay as we are,' replied Stephanie firmly, helping her to sort the blooms. 'I like our arrangement. We live together, we share the house, and I don't have to worry about his mother breathing down my neck, grumbling because I'm not pregnant like Tom's wife, Lesley.' She picked up a rich red carnation and sniffed its delicate fragrance. 'Mmm, these are gorgeous, Rach. And don't think I don't know you're trying to change the subject. I'll shut up—I will—so long as you stop kidding yourself. Gabe Webb didn't buy all these

flowers for you to decorate the café with them. I'm telling
you, it's you he's interested in. Just don't let him hurt you,
right? I haven't forgotten that if it wasn't for him you and
Andrew might still be together.'

We wouldn't.

But Rachel didn't say the words out loud. She had no
desire to arouse her friend's sympathy by telling her what
Andrew had said about Hannah, or that Gabriel had had nothing to do with his son's prejudices. She might never need to
do so, after all. This casual liaison with Gabriel was never
going to lead anywhere, and, as Stephanie had said, she had
no intention of allowing either of the Webbs to hurt her
again.

'You know,' Stephanie added, just when Rachel had
thought the subject was closed, 'you do have to wonder what
he's playing at. He stopped Andrew from seeing you, yet he
seems to see nothing wrong in pursuing you himself.'

On Saturday, Rachel took the afternoon off so that she and
Hannah could attend the craft fair at St Agnes's Church. Her
daughter loved these fairs, where you could buy anything
from home-made cakes and pastries to handcrafted ornaments
and embroidered quilts. And, because the stalls were all low
enough for her to see from her wheelchair, they had an added
appeal.

They were trying to decide which coloured sweater
Hannah liked best when Rachel became aware of someone
standing behind her. Her daughter was of a similar colouring
to herself, and the two patterned woollens, one in blue and
one in green, were each a work of art.

'I'd go for the green one if I were you, Hannah,' remarked
a familiar voice, and Rachel glanced round to find Joe Collins
smiling at the little girl.

'Do you think so?' For all her usual reticence with men,
Hannah was not above a trace of vanity. Holding the green
sweater against her chest, she drew her long braid of hair

forward so that it lay against the emerald-green wool. 'It is pretty, isn't it, Mummy? Do you like it?'

'I like them both,' said Rachel candidly, hoping Joe hadn't got some intention of joining them. A hope that seemed to be dashed when he squatted down beside the child's wheel-chair.

'So how are you, Hannah?' he asked, and the little girl looked doubtfully up at her mother.

'Um—I'm fine,' she said at last. Then, 'Can I have the green sweater, Mummy? I think I do like it best.'

'You've got good taste. Just like your mummy,' said Joe, undaunted by Hannah's indifference. 'So—are you going to splash out and spend some of your pocket money?'

Hannah's smile was diffident. 'Mummy buys my clothes, not me.'

'Who said anything about clothes?' asked Joe, getting to his feet and looking at Rachel. 'I was thinking of an ice cream.' He put his hand into his pocket and pulled out a handful of change. 'Here you are. You go and get us all a sugar cone. I'm sure Mrs Miller's daughter will carry them back for you, if you ask her nicely.'

'No…' Rachel's hand cut between them, blocking any attempt Hannah might have made to take the money. 'Hannah's just had an ice cream, haven't you, sweetheart? She doesn't need another one.'

Joe mouth tightened. 'It's only an ice cream, Rachel. Even if she has had one already, I doubt if another will make that much difference.'

'It wasn't an ice cream,' put in Hannah, though she seemed unaffected by her mother's decision. 'It was an ice lolly, wasn't it, Mummy? You had one, too.'

'So I did—'

'Well, if you won't let me buy the child an ice cream, perhaps you'll let me take her across to see my mother,' suggested Joe doggedly. 'She's running the hat stall over there.' He waved somewhat vaguely in the direction of the door. 'I know she'd love to meet her.'

Rachel wanted to say no, but she didn't want to offend him, so, bending down to Hannah's level, she said, 'Is that what you'd like to do?'

'Just go to another stall?' asked Hannah anxiously. 'We wouldn't have to go in a car or anything, would we?'

'No,' said Rachel gently. 'Joe's just going to wheel you across the hall. He wants to introduce you to his mummy. Is that all right?'

Hannah still looked doubtful, but Joe was so eager Rachel didn't have the heart to refuse. 'It'll be fun, darling,' she said, hoping no one would jump to the wrong conclusion. The last thing she wanted was for people to link her and Joe together.

He wheeled her daughter away, but not without a telling glance in Rachel's direction. She knew he was thinking that she was to blame for Hannah's reticence, that it was she who was afraid of allowing another man into either of their lives.

If he only knew!

Rachel paid for the green sweater and then, deciding there was no point in worrying over it, she drifted on to the used bookstall. Although it wasn't the usual thing to find at a craft fair, St Agnes's had so many books donated for their jumble sales that they inevitably inserted a book stall whenever possible, using the funds earned to sponsor beds at the town's hospice. Some of the books were so old and dog-eared that Rachel was loath to touch them, but here and there were vintage editions of the classics and moderately new paperbacks.

She was flicking through the pages of an old Rupert Bear annual that she thought Hannah might like when, once again, she got the feeling that someone was watching her. Lifting her head, she glanced around, half expecting to see Joe and Hannah coming back. But they had disappeared into the throng. Instead, her eyes were drawn to the double doors that led into the church hall—and the man who was standing just inside them, looking in her direction.

It was Gabriel Webb, and even as she felt the familiar flutter of panic in her stomach that his appearance always evoked, his attention was distracted. Father Michael, one of the priests from the hospice, had recognised him and, judging from the way he was smiling and shaking Gabriel's hand, his arrival was not unexpected.

Which was just as well, thought Rachel firmly, returning her attention to the book in her hand. She could do without the aggravation that seeing him again would cause, and with Hannah present there would be no way she could keep it a secret.

Not that she'd made a very good job of keeping things secret so far, she reflected wryly, handing the annual to the volunteer who was running the stall for pricing. When her mother and Hannah had come into the café, after her daughter's physiotherapy on Thursday afternoon, the first thing Mrs Redfern had noticed were the flowers. And, of course, Rachel hadn't been able to explain their appearance without admitting that she'd had a drink with Gabriel on Wednesday evening after work. Which had caused another argument with her mother. She'd been almost relieved when he hadn't returned on either Thursday or Friday to check on their delivery. Life became far too complicated when he was around.

But what was he doing here?

'Mummy, Mummy!' Hannah's excited voice made the question irrelevant, and Rachel turned to see that her daughter was now sporting a wide-brimmed straw boater. A red and white striped scarf encircled the crown of the hat and trailed down onto the little girl's shoulder. 'Look what Mrs Collins gave me!' she beamed.

'It's very smart.' Rachel smiled, her eyes drifting up briefly to Joe's wary face. 'Did you thank Mrs Collins?'

'Of course.' Hannah was indignant, twisting her head to see her reflection in a hand-painted mirror on an adjoining

stall. She preened for a moment and then her eyes widened
and she lifted her hand to wave at someone she could see in
the glass. 'Look, Mummy,' she pointed. 'There's Mr Webb.'

'Webb?' whispered Joe in Rachel's ear. 'God, Rachel,
Andrew's not come back, has he?'

'It's his father,' said Rachel in a hurried undertone, aware
that Gabriel was now advancing on them from across the hall.
She hoped she'd be able to control her expression. 'You
know—Gabriel Webb. You knew that he was back.'

'What the hell's he doing here?' snapped Joe, but thankfully Rachel wasn't obliged to find an answer. The older man,
tall and disturbingly familiar in his dark trousers and jacket,
a fine grey cashmere sweater exposed by the hands he'd
pushed into his trouser pockets, had joined them, and she had
enough to do handling her own reaction to his presence.

'Have you come to buy some more flowers?' asked
Hannah at once, with unexpected candour, and Gabriel
looked down at her with amused eyes.

'No,' he said gently, his gaze flicking speculatively between Joe and Rachel. 'Did you like them?'

'I did. I think Mummy did, too,' replied Hannah artlessly.
'But Grandma was cross. She said—'

'That will do, Hannah.' Rachel interrupted her before she
could say anything more embarrassing. 'And—and they were
lovely, Mr Webb, but you shouldn't have bothered.'

'It was no bother,' Gabriel assured her, his eyes raking her
flushed face. He paused, and then added politely, 'I hope
you're enjoying the fair.'

'I wouldn't have thought it was your thing, Mr Webb,'
remarked Joe a little belligerently, evidently resenting his familiarity with Rachel, and Gabriel shrugged.

'I told Father Michael I'd call in,' he said mildly, though
he must have sensed the younger man's antagonism. 'I see
you've found something you like, Mrs Kershaw.'

'Oh, yes…'

Rachel was about to tell Hannah about the annual when

the little girl surprisingly intervened. 'Do you like my hat, Mr Webb?' she asked, apparently feeling no threat from his direction. 'Joe's mummy gave it to me. She's got a hat stall, you see.'

Gabriel's lips tilted. 'It's very—sophisticated,' he said at last. 'I like the scarf. It suits you.'

Hannah turned back to the mirror again, content to admire her reflection, and for a few moments there was a strained silence. Then, as if he'd decided that his presence was causing a problem, Gabriel excused himself on the pretext of promising to speak to the volunteers. He strolled away, and he hadn't gone more than a few yards before he was joined by two of the women from the Young Wives Group who had organised the event. His courteous smile appeared, encompassing them in its warmth, and Rachel suddenly felt an entirely different emotion: jealousy.

'Good riddance,' said Joe harshly, as soon as Gabriel was out of earshot, and Rachel remembered belatedly that Joe's father had worked for the pharmaceutical company before being made redundant. It probably explained at least some of his antipathy towards him, and she tried to be charitable when he continued, 'And what was all that about him sending you flowers? I didn't know you knew him that well.'

'I told you he'd come into the café,' protested Rachel defensively, and then chided herself for allowing him that privilege. 'In any case, I don't know why you were rude to him. He was only being polite.'

'Polite, my—' Joe bit off the expletive for Hannah's sake and scowled. 'You're not telling me he gives a damn about you?'

Rachel glanced swiftly in her daughter's direction, afraid she might have heard what he'd said, but happily the little girl was now talking to the woman who was in charge of the mirror stall. Hannah had no trouble talking to women, but Rachel had been surprised when she'd spoken to Gabriel.

'Anyway, if he turns up again I'd tell him to get lost, if I were you,' Joe continued, and Rachel heaved a sigh.

'But you're not me,' she said shortly. 'I run a café, Joe. I can't pick and choose my customers.'

'What?' Joe stared at her. 'Are you saying you've never refused to serve anyone?' He paused. 'What about those two youths who rolled out of the Golden Lion as you were closing that afternoon? You refused to serve them.'

'They were drunk,' cried Rachel impatiently. She caught her tongue between her teeth. 'Gab—Mr Webb wasn't drunk. I had no reason to refuse to serve him.'

'Not even the fact that he didn't consider you good enough to go out with his son?'

'Oh, Joe!' Rachel stifled a groan. 'I told you the other day, I don't care about Andrew or his—his—' She had been going to say prejudices, but now she thought again. 'Or his father,' she declared, not altogether truthfully. 'Now, can we change the subject, please?'

'Suits me.' Joe shrugged. 'I was only thinking of you.'

'I know.' And she did. But Rachel decided it was time she and Hannah left. Putting her hands on her daughter's shoulders, she bent to bestow a light kiss on the top of her head. 'Time to go, sweetheart,' she said. 'I told Steph I'd be there before closing time. I have to collect the keys. I need them to open up on Monday morning.'

'Oh, Mummy...'

'I'll walk along with you, if you like,' offered Joe at once, but Rachel had no intention of fuelling his illusion that they could be more than friends.

'No, you stay, Joe,' she said firmly, her eyes reinforcing the message in her words, and he exhaled heavily.

'I'm leaving anyway.'

'We'll see you later,' insisted Rachel, grasping the wheelchair tightly and propelling it away across the floor. 'Bye, Joe.'

It wasn't easy to make a dignified exit, with the aisles

between the stalls busy with customers, but somehow she made it. She breathed a sigh of relief when they emerged from the building, and not even Hannah's complaint that she hadn't seen half the stalls deterred her.

She hadn't seen Gabriel as she'd manoeuvred Hannah's chair through the throng of visitors, but several people had recognised her and stopped what they were doing to speak to Hannah. Conscious that Joe might be right behind them, Rachel had cut these exchanges short, making her excuses with a guilty tongue.

It was only a matter of a few hundred yards between the church hall and Slater Street, where the café was situated. Although the sky was overcast, the rain had held off, and it was a fairly warm afternoon for early May. Hurrying along, Rachel was glad she was only wearing a cropped sleeveless top and a short khaki skirt. Her hair, which was slightly longer than she usually wore it, had been looped back behind her ears, but damp tendrils escaped to brush her cheeks and invade the corner of her mouth.

She became aware of the car beside her almost at the same moment that Hannah noticed it, too. The sleek grey Mercedes matched its pace to theirs, and Rachel knew without looking who it must be.

'It's Mr Webb,' said Hannah anxiously, as the chauffeur stopped the car and Gabriel got out. She looked up at her mother with wide nervous eyes. 'He's not going to ask us to get in the car, is he?'

Rachel shook her head. 'No,' she said definitely. Then, glancing sideways, 'I don't know what he wants.'

'I think he wants to speak to you, Mummy,' declared Hannah, chewing on her lip. 'He's following us.'

Rachel sighed. She wasn't at all sure she wanted to speak to him again either. After the way Joe had behaved, she was loath to give anyone, particularly her mother, any more ammunition to use against her, especially as she still wasn't sure if she trusted him. But Hannah was bound to mention that they'd spoken to Gabriel at the craft fair, and Mrs Redfern might get suspicious if she heard that Rachel had been stand-offish now. So: there was no harm in speaking to him. Was there?

CHAPTER FIVE

RACHEL'S feet slowed almost automatically, making it easy for Gabriel to catch up with them, and he looked down at Hannah with a very different smile from the one he'd given the women at the craft fair. 'I bet you're going to your mother's café to have another of those delicious sundaes, aren't you?' he said lightly. 'Do you think she'd mind if I came, too?'

Hannah hesitated, and Gabriel looked at Rachel then, his eyes challenging her to refuse him. And, although she tried to kindle her anger and accuse him of using the child to gain his own ends, she couldn't do it. Despite his confident words there was wary uncertainty in his dark gaze, and she felt her stomach quiver in unwilling anticipation.

'You're welcome to join us if you want to, isn't he, Hannah?' she asked, including the little girl in her decision, and Hannah's smile appeared again.

'You—you can even push my chair, if you like,' she offered cautiously, and Rachel wondered if Gabriel was aware of the importance of that concession. Hannah had rarely, if ever, volunteered that anyone but Rachel, her mother, or one of the care-workers from her school should push her wheel-chair.

It brought a lump to Rachel's throat and, as if sensing the honour he had been granted, Gabriel lifted a hand as if to stroke her cheek. But then, apparently thinking better of it, he turned back to the wheelchair and the little girl who was watching his every move.

'I'd be delighted,' he said, gesturing to his chauffeur to drive on, and Rachel moved aside so that he could take her place.

His fingers brushed hers as he took charge of the wheel-chair, and although his hands were cool, and should have been impersonal, Rachel felt a jolt of electricity spring between them. The heat of his touch seemed to burn the length of her arm and her fingers moved instinctively to protect herself.

Gabriel's eyes darkened as he looked at her, and she wondered if he had experienced the same shock of awareness that she had. But surely a man like Gabriel Webb wouldn't get excited just because he'd touched a woman's hand, she chided herself. How naïve she must seem.

'What happened to your escort?'

Gabriel was speaking and Rachel forced herself to concentrate on what he was saying. 'Joe wasn't my escort,' she said, a little stiffly. And then, because she didn't want him to think she felt the need to convince him, she added, 'I mean—he's just a friend. We didn't go to the fair together.'

'I'm glad.' Gabriel spoke softly. 'He obviously doesn't like the fact that he's got some competition.'

Rachel stared at him. 'You are joking, of course.'

'No, I'm not.' Gabriel shook his head. 'Rachel, why is it so hard for you to believe that I find you attractive? You're a beautiful woman. And—' his lips twisted '—despite my advanced years, I still have the usual male urges, however shocking that might sound to you.'

Rachel caught her breath. 'You shouldn't say things like that in—in front of Hannah,' she whispered, and his lips curved into a devastating smile.

'Is it all right if I say them when we're alone together?' he enquired mockingly, and Rachel's face burned.

'What are you talking about?' asked Hannah, before she could think of a reply. The little girl looked up at them with indignant eyes. 'I can't hear you. Grandma says it's rude to whisper when other people are there.'

'We weren't whispering,' lied Rachel breathily, aware that

Hannah would relate everything that had happened to her grandmother. 'Um—Mr Webb was just saying that—that—'

'I was wondering what your grandmother will think of your new hat,' put in Gabriel coolly, and Rachel flashed him an incredulous look. Trust him to have a ready answer, she thought, not without a certain amount of envy. 'Will you be wearing it for school?' he went on easily. 'If so, I'm sure all the boys are going to be dazzled by your beauty.'

Hannah giggled. 'Do you think I'm beautiful?' she exclaimed delightedly, and Rachel gave him a warning look.

'Sure you are, sweetcakes,' he assured her, his eyes moving briefly to Rachel's mouth. 'You're going to dazzle all the boys when you grow up.'

Hannah pursed her lips. 'I don't have anything to do with boys,' she said firmly, and Gabriel frowned.

'Why not?'

'I hope it's not going to rain,' put in Rachel, wanting to change the subject, but Hannah wasn't listening to her.

'I don't like boys,' she said. 'They're too rough.'

'Was that a spot of rain?' Rachel tried to quicken the pace. 'What a good job Grandma's coming to pick us up. We don't want to get wet, do we?'

'Who says boys are too rough?' persisted Gabriel, as indifferent to Rachel's pleas as her daughter, and she sighed.

'Does it matter?' she exclaimed, giving him a telling look. 'Here's the café. Are you coming in?'

'Is that an invitation?' he asked, at last responding to her efforts to divert the conversation, and Rachel gave an awkward nod.

'If you like,' she said, going ahead of them to open the door. 'It looks like we just got here in time.'

It did indeed start to rain in earnest as they entered the café, and Rachel hurried across to speak to Stephanie as Gabriel wheeled Hannah's chair to one of the many unoccupied tables. At this hour of the afternoon there were only a couple of customers left, sitting at the table near the door, and they stared at Hannah with openly pitying eyes.

Rachel noticed this as Stephanie came through from the kitchen to see who had come in, and her blood boiled at their lack of sensitivity. Hadn't they ever seen a child in a wheelchair before? Didn't they understand that the last thing Hannah needed was for people to treat her as an oddity?

'Is that who I think it is?' asked Stephanie in a hushed voice as Gabriel turned his back on them to speak to Hannah, and Rachel nodded.

'I expect so,' she said drily. 'How are things? Did you manage okay?'

'Yeah, no problem.' But Stephanie couldn't seem to drag her eyes away from Gabriel. 'How come?'

'How come what?'

Stephanie pulled a wry face. 'Like you don't know.'

'Oh—he was at the craft fair,' said Rachel offhandedly. 'He walked back with us.'

'Just like that?'

'More or less.' Rachel glanced around. 'Where's Patsy?'

'I let her go about half an hour ago,' replied her friend carelessly. 'Will you be having tea?'

Rachel hesitated. 'I guess so. But don't you worry, Steph. I can get it. You can go, if you like. I can close up.'

'What? And miss seeing you and *him* together?' Stephanie grimaced. 'Not likely.'

'Oh, Steph—' Rachel began, and then broke off at the sight of Gabriel lifting Hannah out of her chair. 'What the hell does he think he's doing?'

'Wait!' Stephanie caught her arm as she would have charged towards them. 'Look, he's putting her on one of the ordinary chairs, that's all. And, judging by Hannah's expression, she doesn't have any objections.'

It was true. Hannah's arms had been around Gabriel's neck as he lifted her, and now she sat on one of the café chairs, beaming at him. Her dangling legs looked paler than normal perhaps, but Rachel realised that, looking at her now, no one would suspect she was paralysed.

'Why do you think he's done that?' she said, half to herself, but Stephanie heard her.

'I imagine because it's one in the eye for those two over there,' she muttered, glaring at the man and woman who had stared as they came in. 'Condescending bastards! They should know better.'

Andrew didn't, thought Rachel ruefully, but thankfully this time she kept her words to herself. 'I'll get the tea,' she said, and lifted a china teapot down from the upper shelf.

'I'll go and see if Hannah wants a milkshake, shall I?' suggested Stephanie slyly, and Rachel gave an exasperated smile.

'All right,' she said. 'If you must. But don't say anything unpleasant, please!'

'As if I would,' exclaimed Stephanie indignantly, and sauntered away.

She was back a few minutes later, her fair cheeks flushed with becoming colour. 'God, he's sexy, isn't he?' she hissed, brushing past Rachel to take a carton of milk from the fridge. 'No wonder you won't have a word said against him!'

'Steph!'

'Well, it's true, isn't it?' Stephanie poured milk into the blender. 'I mean, I don't blame you. Sexy and rich! What an irresistible combination!'

Rachel expelled a weary breath. 'I'm not interested in his money.'

'Does that mean you are interested in him?' Stephanie arched a mocking brow. 'Of course you are. There's no point in denying it.' She paused. 'Are you sleeping with him?'

'No!' Rachel was horrified, and she cast an anxious look in Gabriel's direction. But he couldn't possibly have heard, she reassured herself, before continuing, 'For God's sake, Steph, we hardly know one another.'

'Are you sure?' Stephanie wasn't convinced. 'That was some bouquet of flowers he sent you.'

'I'm not going to listen to this.' Rachel began setting cups and saucers on a tray. 'He—he's far too old for me. You said it yourself.'

'No, I didn't.' Stephanie added strawberry purée to the milk and set the blender going. 'I was fairly blasé about his age. And what was it you said? There's seventeen years between you? That's nothing nowadays.'

'It's nothing like that,' persisted Rachel, making the tea. 'All right, so he seems to like coming here. So what? He's bored and I'm available—or he thinks I am,' she amended hurriedly. 'I'm not going to delude myself by thinking he's really attracted to me.'

Stephanie gave her a sideways glance. 'Has he said he is?'

Rachel's face burned. 'Please, Steph! Not now.'

'So he has.' Stephanie was admiring. 'Way to go, girl!' She paused. 'Has he told you why he's had to give up his position in the company?'

'No.' Rachel was impatient. Then, curiously, 'How do you know he has?'

'I don't. Not for certain,' admitted Stephanie ruefully. 'But, I mean, if he's having to have medical treatment in Oxford, he's not going to be able to go on running Webb's Pharmaceuticals, is he?'

Rachel's lips tightened. 'You don't know that.'

'Don't I?' Stephanie put her hands on her hips. 'So how come he's able to come in here practically every other day?'

'He doesn't come in here every other day,' exclaimed Rachel shortly. 'And if you tell my mother things like that, no wonder she's always on my back about him.'

'Hey, I've said nothing to your mother since you warned me off,' retorted her friend, looking indignant, and Rachel shook her head.

'Yeah, yeah,' she said. 'I know. And I'm sorry if I'm being touchy again. It's just—it's just—'

'You can't believe he's interested in you,' Stephanie finished for her. 'Well, stranger things have happened. And, if you keep your head, I see no reason why you shouldn't enjoy it.'

'While it lasts?' suggested Rachel wryly, and her friend grimaced.

'You said it. Not me.'

By the time Rachel carried the tray to the table where Gabriel and Hannah were sitting she was feeling quite worn out. Arguing with Stephanie had exhausted her, and Gabriel looked at her a little concernedly as he got up to assist her into the chair.

'Is everything all right?' he asked, in a low voice, and Rachel gave him a resigned look.

'What could be wrong?' she asked, relieved at least that the other two customers had departed in her absence. 'I—Steph was just bringing me up to speed on what's been happening while I've been away.' But she couldn't look at him as she added, 'Sorry to be so long.'

'Gabe's been telling me about his horses,' put in Hannah eagerly, for once neglecting her milkshake in favour of delivering her own piece of news. 'He says that I—'

'Gabe?' broke in Rachel, aghast, and Hannah vigorously nodded her head.

'That's right,' she exclaimed, not immediately noticing her mother's expression. 'He says we can go and see them, and maybe even give them a lump of sugar...'

'Hannah!' Rachel spoke harshly, grasping her daughter's arm with unknowing force. 'Calm down, can't you?' And when the little girl yelped in protest, 'Oh—sorry, sorry.' She shook her head, relaxing her grip, and Hannah pulled away. 'Who gave you permission to call Mr Webb—Gabe?'

'I did,' said Gabriel mildly, resuming his seat. 'I wish you'd call me that, too.'

'What I call you or don't call you isn't at issue here,' said Rachel stiffly, forced into an involuntary glance in his direction. Then, turning back to Hannah, 'And I don't think we can presume upon Mr Webb's good nature by taking him up on his offer.'

'But, Mummy—'

'I believe riding is considered good exercise for para—for children who can't walk,' remarked Gabriel flatly, deliberately choosing words he knew Hannah would understand. 'But obviously I'm not suggesting Hannah should attempt anything like that. Not yet, at any rate.'

Rachel met his gaze with angry eyes. 'And you'd know all about it, I suppose?'

'I didn't say that.'

'No, but you've said enough to raise a little girl's hopes without even mentioning it to me, let alone taking my feelings into account,' exclaimed Rachel fiercely. 'You had no right to do that.'

Gabriel blew out a breath. 'Okay. Point taken. I should have discussed it with you first.'

'Yes, you should.'

He inclined his head. 'I'm sorry.'

'So may I go, Mummy?'

'No.'

'Why not?' Hannah's face had crumpled. 'What's wrong with going and seeing the horses? I've never seen a horse up close before.'

Rachel's jaws ground together. 'Gabe' had said altogether too much, she thought furiously. She should never have left Hannah alone with him. She should have known when he lifted her out of the wheelchair that he was getting far too involved in their lives.

'Is it okay if I go now?'

Stephanie's voice had a curiously upsetting effect on Rachel. Suddenly she was aware of how unreasonable she was being, and, meeting her friend's speculative gaze, she had no doubt that Stephanie had decided to get out before she turned her anger on her.

'Of course,' Rachel said now, but her voice still betrayed the tension she was trying so hard to conceal. 'Um—see you on Monday.'

'Right.' Stephanie nodded and then, tugging on the little girl's braid, ''Bye, Hannah.' She didn't speak to Gabriel, but she did cast a small smile in his direction before sauntering casually to the door.

It slammed behind her, the bell tinkling on for several seconds after she'd departed. Rachel didn't know what to say, so she busied herself with setting out the teacups to give herself time to think. But it didn't work. She was no nearer finding a solution when Hannah, who had been staring at her sulkily, said, 'I don't want anything,' in a tearful voice.

'But you said you wanted a milkshake,' protested Rachel. 'You can't waste it.'

'I don't want it,' insisted Hannah, turning her head away. 'I want to go home.'

'Oh, God!'

'Why are you so angry, Rachel?' It was Gabriel who spoke now, and she felt the colour pouring into her cheeks again. 'Don't blame the child because you're angry with me.'

'I'm not angry with you,' she mumbled untruthfully, grateful that for the moment Hannah didn't appear to be listening to them, and Gabriel gave her a retiring look.

'Aren't you?'

'Why should I be?' She countered his question with one of her own and he gave a wry smile.

'Because you resent me talking to your daughter?' he suggested. 'Because you don't think I should have lifted her out of her chair?' He paused, and then added softly, 'Or because your friend thought we might be sleeping together?'

Rachael's jaw dropped. 'You heard what she said?'

'When the café is empty, voices carry,' he explained simply, and her shoulders rounded.

Then her gaze darted to her daughter. 'Did—did—?'

'I doubt if what was said meant anything to Hannah,' he

assured her, with a shake of his head. 'But, just in case, I distracted her by telling her about my horses.'

Rachel groaned. 'Oh, Lord!' She felt terrible now. 'So that was why you...'

'Not entirely,' he admitted honestly. 'I would like to invite you and Hannah to Copleys. I'm not entirely selfless. I want you to come and see my house, to have lunch with me. And if, after I've seduced you with good food and wine, we should make our way down to the stables, then both Hannah and myself would have something to look forward to.'

'Oh, yes, Mummy.' Clearly Hannah had heard this, and her head swung round instantly. 'Can we go to Copleys? Can we? Can we? Please! Please!'

'May we,' corrected Rachel automatically, but her eyes were held by Gabriel's dark compelling gaze. 'I—don't know.'

'Oh, Mummy!'

Rachel was aware of Hannah staring frustratedly at her, but she couldn't help it. She kept hearing that word *seduced*, and its associations had nothing to do with food or wine or horses. It spelled silk sheets and sex, and danger, and she was very much afraid he was seducing her.

'Why—why would you want us to come to Copleys?' she protested huskily. 'Your mother lives there, doesn't she? Won't she object?'

'Copleys belongs to me,' he told her gently.

'Even so...'

'Rachel, you know why I want you to accept my invitation.' He expelled a longish sigh. 'But don't worry. It doesn't commit you to anything but a couple of hours in my company.' He paused. 'If you'd rather not come—'

'I—I didn't say that.'

'So what are you saying?'

'I don't know.'

And that was the truth. Rachel didn't know what she was saying, what she wanted to say. The idea of going to Copleys was so unexpected—so outrageous—she couldn't think of anything else.

'Well, I just want you to know that if you can't accept then I'll have to live with it,' he remarked quietly. 'But, please, don't insult me by pretending you think I feel some kind of obligation towards you for the way Andrew behaved. I don't. This is between us. No one else.'

Rachel poured the tea with a trembling hand, pushing his cup towards him because she was afraid that if she picked it up she might humiliate herself completely by dropping it. This couldn't be happening, she thought weakly. A man like Gabriel Webb, a man as influential and wealthy as Gabriel Webb, didn't get involved with a woman like her. He didn't. It was as she had said to Stephanie: he was bored, that was all, looking for a diversion, and it was amusing him right now to turn her world upside-down.

And yet...

'Can we—*may* we go, Mummy, please?' Hannah begged again, and Rachel felt dizzy with the knowledge that she wanted to say yes.

CHAPTER SIX

IT WAS just as well that Rachel got up early on Sunday morning. She had breakfast to prepare—her mother had apparently gone on strike for the day—and an excited Hannah to bathe and get ready before she even started on herself. Which wasn't easy when the little girl persisted in delaying matters by asking dozens of questions that Rachel couldn't answer. But telling Hannah that she knew no more about Copleys than her daughter did didn't seem to get through to her, and Rachel didn't want to spoil the day by being a total wet blanket.

All the same, it wasn't easy keeping up her spirits when her mother came downstairs to have breakfast with them and proceeded to tell her once again what a fool she was being for letting *that man* into their lives. Mrs Redfern had already made her feelings clear at supper the previous evening, when Hannah had blithely told her about how they'd met *Gabe* at the craft fair and how he'd come to the café to have tea with them.

Thankfully, she'd saved the worst of her comments until after Hannah had gone to bed, but this morning she had evidently decided that the little girl deserved to know that her grandmother did not approve of this outing. Refusing the scrambled eggs Rachel had prepared, she poured herself a cup of coffee before launching her latest tirade.

'You do realise he's only using you, Rachel, don't you?' she demanded. 'As soon as he's fit again he'll be beating a path back to London, and you'll be left high and dry. I can't believe you can't see it for yourself! After your experience with Andrew, I'd have thought you'd have steered clear of any member of the Webb family.'

'Oh, Mum!' Rachel sank down into the seat opposite, the slice of toast she had prepared for herself suddenly too much for her to swallow. 'He's not like that.'

'Who? *Gabe?*' Her mother said his name with scornful emphasis. 'Why don't you use his name? Obviously that's what you call him when you're together.'

'It—' Rachel broke off. She had been about to say, *It isn't*, but she refused to give her mother that satisfaction. 'It's my life,' she said instead, and Mrs Redfern glared at her.

'It's not just your life, Rachel. It's Hannah's and mine, as well. You can say what you like, but it isn't fair to let her think that the kind of life Gabriel Webb leads is normal. Taking her to that big house, letting her feed his damn horses! She'll be getting big ideas that you can't possibly satisfy, and then I'll have to pick up the pieces. Again. It's crazy, and you know it.'

'What's crazy?' Hannah was looking anxious now, and Rachel heaved a sigh.

'Nothing, sweetheart,' she said reassuringly. Then, to her mother, 'I don't want to talk about it any more. Not here; not now.'

Mrs Redfern shrugged, but thankfully she didn't pursue it, and Rachel checked that Hannah was getting on with her breakfast before getting to her feet.

'I'm going to get ready,' she said, encompassing both of them in her tight smile. 'I won't be long.'

In fact, she was longer than she'd intended. It wasn't easy trying to choose something to wear, and she dressed and undressed a dozen times before deciding on a deep brown linen trouser suit that she wore with a thin yellow shirt. The colours gave warmth to her fair skin, and with her hair pushed back behind a matching linen band she thought she looked reasonably ready for anything.

Except for the man who had invited them, she amended tensely, painting her mouth with an earthy-tinted pigment.

She doubted she would ever be ready for him, but her stomach clenched with an excitement she didn't want to feel.

Downstairs again, she saw that Hannah had been crying, and she looked accusingly at her mother, waiting for an explanation. But, although Mrs Redfern was wearing a guilty expression, it was the little girl who spoke.

'Grandma says that I'll have to go in—in Mr Webb's car,' she said tearfully. 'I don't want to go in Mr Webb's car. You said you would be coming, Mummy.'

'I am,' said Rachel urgently, sinking down onto her haunches beside the little girl's chair. 'And I told you, we're going in our car.' She looked up at her mother with angry eyes. 'Grandma's got it wrong.'

'D'you mean to say he expects you to make your own way there?' exclaimed the older woman scornfully. 'I would have thought the least he could do was send a car for you. Still, I suppose it just goes to prove what he really thinks about—'

'He offered,' Rachel broke in sharply, getting to her feet and handing Hannah a tissue to blow her nose. 'But I said I preferred to drive us. For obvious reasons,' she added, as the child emitted another sob. 'I wish you'd mind your own business, Mum, I really do.'

'Oh, I will.' Mrs Redfern got to her feet now, and wrapped the dressing gown she was wearing closer about her. 'From now on I won't say a word about it. If you want to make a fool of yourself, go ahead! It won't be the first time, will it?'

She turned then and left the room, and Rachel heaved another sigh. All she really wanted to do now was abandon the whole outing. The day had started so badly she couldn't believe it could possibly improve, and the prospect of meeting Gabriel's mother loomed large on the horizon. What if she was just like her own mother, only worse? What would she do?

'We really are going in our car?' Hannah asked, tugging her sleeve, and Rachel realised that she couldn't possibly change her mind. Hannah was looking forward to this, God help her, and she had to remember she had only agreed to it for the child's sake. Or, at least, that was what she had been telling herself ever since she'd accepted Gabriel's invitation.

It took Rachel about twenty minutes to reach the gates of Copleys. They were closed at first, but they opened at their approach, and she guessed there was a hidden camera somewhere, whose operator monitored all visitors.

Which didn't give her any encouragement. What kind of people were these, who lived behind electrically operated gates and who employed personnel whose sole occupation was guarding their security?

She swallowed hard, and as they progressed up the long winding drive even Hannah began to look a little apprehensive. They suddenly seemed a long way from home, and her mother's warnings were all too relevant.

The house itself reassured her. Although it was every bit as big and impressive as she had expected, it was also built of a mellow Cotswold brick that was liberally laced with climbing wisteria. Long casement windows flanked a centre entrance that was approached up a shallow flight of steps, and above them tall chimneys were familiar and homely against a sky that had cleared as soon as they left Maple Avenue.

'It's a big house,' said Hannah doubtfully, as the Mondeo crunched over a gravelled forecourt, and Rachel thought that was the understatement of the year.

'Some people have big houses,' she said, in the hope of diminishing its importance in Hannah's eyes, but it didn't work.

'I've never seen such a big house before,' she declared worriedly. 'Do lots of people live here?'

'I hope not,' muttered Rachel inaudibly, and then, for the child's benefit, 'Not a lot.' She stopped the car and sat for a few moments, trying to gather her composure. Then, thrusting open her door, she said, 'Okay. Let's do it.'

'Do what?' protested Hannah, frowning as her mother went round to the rear of the estate car to get her wheelchair, and Rachel forced a smile.

'Go and knock at the door, of course,' she said brightly, wishing she'd never agreed to come here. She hoisted out the chair and, adjusting it, wheeled it round to Hannah's door. 'Here we are. Let's get you out.'

'I can do that.'

Gabriel's breath was warm on the side of her neck and Rachel turned in surprise to find he was standing just a few inches away. 'Where did you come from?' she asked, before she could stop herself, and his lips twitched.

'Well, I didn't materialise out of the air,' he remarked drily. He gestured behind him and now she saw the heavy door was standing open. Another black-clad figure was standing at the top of the flight of steps, and Rachel realised she had been so intent on getting this over with that she hadn't been aware of anyone else. 'I—was waiting for you.'

'You mean someone else was,' mumbled Rachel ungraciously, and Gabriel gave a careless shrug.

'I'm not going to argue with you,' he said, bending to speak to the child. 'Hello, Hannah. How are you today?'

'I'm all right.' But Hannah still looked anxious. Then, uncertainly, 'Is this really your house?'

'I'm afraid so.' Gabriel gave a half smile. 'Don't you like it?'

'It's very big,' said Hannah doubtfully. 'Are there lots of rooms?'

'Lots,' agreed Gabriel good-humouredly. 'Now, are you going to let me lift you out?'

Hannah hesitated, looking up at her mother for guidance. But Rachel wasn't about to say anything in their host's favour, and after a moment the little girl said, 'All right. But Grandma says I'm very heavy.'

Gabriel exchanged a brief look with Rachel then, and she was fairly sure he was thinking *Grandma would*. But cour-

tesy won out, and without another word he bent and plucked
the child, who was anything but heavy, from her seat and
deposited her in the wheelchair.

'There we are,' he said, straightening and flexing his spine.
He grimaced. 'I don't think I've done any permanent dam-
age.'

Hannah giggled. 'I'm not that heavy!' She glanced up at
her mother, expecting to include her in the joke, and noticed
her tight face. 'What's wrong? Why are you looking so
cross?'

'I'm not cross.' Rachel gave an inward groan. There was
no chance of being subtle where Hannah was concerned.

'Your mummy is having doubts about coming here,' said
Gabriel with equal candour. 'Perhaps she doesn't like my
house either.'

'I like it,' protested Hannah staunchly. 'I do. I think it's
lovely.'

'And so do I,' put in Rachel shortly. 'I just don't know
what we're doing here.'

'You're here because I invited you,' replied Gabriel
mildly. 'Now, come on. We'll join my mother for morning
coffee before I take Hannah to see the stables.'

Rachel hesitated, her mouth drying. 'Your mother!'

'I do have one,' agreed Gabriel lightly. 'And I used to
have a father, too, believe it or not. Don't worry. You may
like her.'

Rachel shook her head a little dazedly, her fingers moving
revealingly from the hem of her jacket to the seam of her
trousers, and Gabriel's eyes softened.

'You look beautiful,' he said huskily, his eyes on her
mouth. 'You both do,' he added, taking in Hannah's pretty
flowered trousers and pink denim jerkin. 'I'm a very fortu-
nate man.'

Rachel pursed her lips, meeting his gaze with mutinous
eyes, but once again Hannah saved the day. 'May Gabe push

my chair, Mummy?' she asked, and there was no way her mother could refuse.

'Why not?' she conceded, but there was still an edge to her voice and Gabriel heard it.

'Relax,' he advised gently, before taking charge of the wheelchair and starting towards the steps.

It was all right for him, thought Rachel irritably, crunching over the gravelled drive after them. This was his house, his land, his territory. He was perfectly at ease here. Even the black silk shirt he was wearing, the sleeves rolled back over forearms lightly covered with coarse dark hair, fairly screamed its designer label. It exposed the unexpected width of his shoulders, too, his close-fitting trousers and laced deck shoes giving him the kind of unconscious sophistication that was impossible to simulate.

Not that he needed to simulate anything, she reflected edgily. As Stephanie had said, he was a millionaire several times over, and inviting her and Hannah to lunch at Copleys was probably just his way of salving his social conscience.

The man who had been waiting for them at the top of the steps came down to help Gabriel lift Hannah's chair into the porch. He was obviously an employee of some kind, and Rachel wasn't surprised when Gabriel introduced him as Joseph, his butler.

'Joseph's been with me more years than I care to remember,' he added ruefully, slapping the other man affectionately on the back. A few years older than his employer—and considerably heavier—Joseph was evidently more than just an employee, and Rachel felt a twinge of shame for her own cynicism. She had to ignore what her mother had said and start being a bit more positive about—about everything.

Beyond the double doors, which Joseph had opened to admit Hannah's chair, an enormous reception hall awaited them. Its cream-painted walls rose more than two floors to an arched atrium which slanted sunlight down on the many paintings that were hung there. Carved oak pillars supported the galleried landing above a curving staircase, and the polished floor was partly covered by a glowing tapestry rug.

'Gosh!'

Hannah, at least, was not ashamed to show her admiration and Rachel murmured, 'Very nice,' with total banality. But what was she supposed to say? she asked herself emotively. Just because it was even more impressive than even she had expected.

'My mother's in the conservatory,' said Gabriel, propelling Hannah's chair across the rug, and Rachel was grateful that he didn't seem to expect any response from her. But, nevertheless, her knees felt a little unsteady as she followed him, and she hoped Joseph, who was closing the doors behind them, wouldn't notice.

The hall might have seemed huge, but they managed to cross it in double-quick time. Although, for the most part, Rachel kept her gaze on Gabriel's back, when her eyes dropped to the tight curve of his buttocks she forced herself to look away. That was not why she was here, she reminded herself, and determinedly glanced about her.

Several doors that opened into the hall were closed, but one was open, exposing a spacious drawing room. A bank of windows gave a glimpse of lawned gardens, while inside the room matching bisque-coloured velvet sofas were set at right angles around a low splay-legged occasional table, where a delicate bronze sculpture glinted in the sunlight.

They left the hall to cross what appeared to be a morning room. A round table and half a dozen matching chairs held a central position, the shining surface of the table reflecting the bowl of fruit that sat in the middle. Side windows gave light to the room, but its main illumination came from the large glass-walled conservatory that adjoined it.

Glass-leaved doors had been folded back, and beyond the green foliage of various palms and climbing plants a dark-haired woman was sitting on a cushioned rattan sofa, reading a newspaper. Several other chairs and sofas flanked a glass-topped table where Rachel guessed it would be fun to have breakfast. But right now she was more concerned with the woman who put the paper aside at their approach and rose to her feet.

Her first impression was that Gabriel's mother was much younger than she'd expected. Or perhaps it was simply the fact of her foreignness. Rachel knew that Mrs Webb had been born in Italy, and it was evident in the vivid colours she wore and in the fact that she hadn't allowed her age to dictate her appearance. Her hair was still as dark as her son's, though it was probably tinted, and her slim-fitting scarlet trousers and paisley-printed shirt accentuated the voluptuous curves of her shapely body. She wore lots of jewellery, too: at least half a dozen gold chains about her neck and several gold bangles on her wrist.

It wasn't easy for Rachel to get her head round the fact that this was Andrew's *grandmother*, and she was feeling a little dazed when the woman took her hand.

'You must be Rachel,' she said, her accent giving the words a delightful intonation. 'I may call you Rachel, *si*? Gabriel has told me so much about you.'

Has he?

Rachel managed to make some polite response, but her mind was buzzing with the realisation that Gabriel had discussed her with his mother. What in God's name had he said?

'And you are Hannah,' continued the older woman, bending to take the little girl's hand in greeting. '*Cara*, you are so pretty! So sweet!' And, as Hannah blossomed, 'But what a pity you have to use this ugly wheelchair! I am sure you must have some other means of getting around, no?'

'Mamma!'

Gabriel spoke warningly, but Rachel cast him a dark look. She didn't need anyone to fight her battles for her, however well meaning he meant to be. Putting a reassuring hand on the child's shoulder, she said, 'Hannah has some crutches, but she prefers not to use them.' Which was a huge under-

statement. Rachel had spent weeks—months—trying to get
the little girl to try them. But it had invariably ended in tears
and eventually Rachel had given up. Now, changing the subject, she said, 'You have a lovely home—er—*signora*.'

'Ah, it is not my home, Rachel,' their hostess replied at
once. 'My home is in Tuscany. Did my son not tell you this?'
She looked to Gabriel for confirmation, but then shrugged. 'I
am a visitor here, just as you are.'

Rachel doubted that. But at least the woman appeared to
have taken the hint, because her next words were harmless
enough. 'Come, sit down, *cara*. I will ring for coffee, *si*?
And what will the little one drink?'

Hannah's jaw was wobbling, as it did when someone had
upset her, and Rachel wished again that she had never accepted Gabriel's invitation. Hannah wasn't used to anyone
making comments about her disability, let alone a total
stranger, and her voice was barely audible as she said, 'A
Coke? Could I have a Coke, Mummy? Would that be all
right?'

'You can have whatever you like,' put in Gabriel, before
Rachel could answer her. He gave his mother a warning look
before adding, 'You can even have a strawberry milkshake,
if you'd prefer it.'

'A Coke will be fine,' declared Rachel tersely, not wanting
to put anyone to any trouble on their behalf. She moved to
take hold of Hannah's chair and Gabriel obediently stepped
aside. 'Thank you.'

'My pleasure,' he said drily, as his mother rang the bell to
summon a member of his staff, but Rachel avoided his eyes
as she wheeled Hannah's chair across the marble-tiled floor
of the conservatory.

Gabriel's mother retreated to the sofa she had been occupying when they arrived, and she indicated that Rachel
should come and sit beside her. However, Rachel had no
desire to get that close to the woman, and, pretending not to
see her outstretched hand, she stationed Hannah's chair be-

side the sofa opposite. Then, subsiding onto the soft cushions, not without some relief, she armoured herself for the inquisition she was sure was to come.

'*E cosi*, we get to meet you at last, Rachel,' the older woman began as soon as Rachel was seated. 'It is a pity we did not meet you before.'

And saved Gabriel the trouble of seeking her out now, Rachel added silently, aware that her hostess was watching her with intent appraising eyes. Despite the apparent warmth of her greeting, she had the feeling that Gabriel's mother had distinct reservations about their association.

But before she could answer, the woman went on, 'Gabriel tells me you are still living in Kingsbridge, no? You live with your mother, *si*? As you did when—'

'Mamma!'

There was no mistaking Gabriel's impatience with her questions now, and the appearance of a uniformed maid provided a welcome break in the conversation. Gabriel himself gave the order for morning coffee, and then strolled across the room to stand beside Hannah's chair.

'So,' he said, squatting down beside her, 'are you looking forward to seeing my horses?'

The little girl's face lifted with sudden excitement. 'Ooh, yes,' she exclaimed, and Rachel guessed that for a few moments the child, too, had forgotten why he had invited them here. Hannah glanced apprehensively at her mother. 'Can we go now?'

'Presently,' promised Gabriel gently, and Rachel was reluctantly reminded that, whatever his mother might say, she had no reason to believe his motives weren't genuine.

All the same, it was obvious his mother was intensely curious about the situation, and Rachel wondered exactly what Andrew had told them about her.

'Do you know, one of the mares had a foal a few days ago?' Gabriel continued now. 'You can help me think of a name for him, if you'd like.'

'Is a foal a baby horse?' asked Hannah, completely absorbed in what he was saying, and Gabriel went on to explain the different names they used for male and female animals.

'Your husband died in a car accident, no?' remarked his mother then, taking advantage of his momentary distraction, and Rachel gave a brief nod.

'That's right,' she said, wondering why the woman considered it necessary to bring that up. 'Three years ago.'

'Three years.' The woman looked thoughtful. 'And your daughter has not walked since then?'

'No.'

Rachel stiffened and glanced swiftly at the child. But Hannah wasn't listening to their conversation. She was too intrigued by what Gabriel was telling her.

'*Che peccato!*' The older woman moved her hands in a sympathetic gesture. 'But she was not injured. What could have happened prior to the crash to cause such a—what is it they say?—trauma? *Si*, trauma.'

'I'd really rather not talk about it—um, *signora*,' said Rachel, unable to think of this woman as *Mrs* Webb.

'*Va bene.*' Belatedly Gabriel's mother drew back from any further questions. 'I did not mean to pry. My son will tell you I am so-o inquisitive.'

Well, that was one way of putting it, thought Rachel, deciding that the woman wasn't half as artless as she'd like to appear. She had her own agenda. There was no doubt about that. And Rachel had the feeling that she and Hannah were unwelcome complications.

Nevertheless, what she'd said about Hannah did trouble Rachel. Although various theories had been put forward as to why the child couldn't—or wouldn't—walk, no one had ever suggested that it might have anything to do with what had happened before the accident. And how could it? Hannah had only been three years old, for heaven's sake!

CHAPTER SEVEN

THE maid returned before anything more could be said. A small woman, in her forties, Rachel estimated, she was wheeling a trolley on which resided cups and saucers, cream and sugar containers, and a tall pot of coffee. There was also a glass of Coke, clinking with ice, for Hannah, and in the warming compartment below were scones already oozing with butter.

Hannah's eyes lit up at the sight of a plate of home-made chocolate chip cookies. She had always loved the crunchy biscuits. In fact, they were one of the few things she had eaten after the accident, when for months she'd turned her face away from other food.

Gabriel rose to his feet with the maid's arrival and helped her to unload the trolley onto the table. Rachel had the feeling this was typical of him, and wondered why she felt she knew him so well. After all, they were hardly close acquaintances. Yet, for all that, she sensed she could trust him, in spite of what her mother had said.

She had cause to revise her opinion a few moments later. To her dismay, he chose to sit beside her, and not beside his mother, and because the sofas weren't large he couldn't help but sit closer to her than she would have wished. So close, in fact, that she could feel the heat of his body along the length of her thigh, couldn't help but inhale the clean male scent of him every time she took a breath.

And she took many breaths during the next few minutes. She was suddenly breathless, her lungs seemingly incapable of absorbing any air. Which was ridiculous, she knew. He was only sitting next to her, for God's sake. If his hip was pressing against hers, he wasn't aware of it. And if she fool-

ishly imagined that he exuded an unconscious sensuality in
everything he did, that was her problem, not his. He was just
a man, after all. An older man than she was used to, perhaps,
but what of it? Surely it was all the more reason for her to
get a hold of herself before he noticed her dilemma. He was
Andrew's father! And she had no difficulty at all in picturing
his reaction if he ever found out what was going on. Dear
Lord, he would never believe that she could be sexually attracted to the man who had sired him.

She suddenly became aware that Gabriel was speaking to
her now, and she was forced to turn her head and look at
him. She had never seen him this close before, and her feelings of apprehension multiplied. God, she could drown in the
dark intensity of his eyes, she thought weakly, hardly aware
of anyone else in that moment. Her mouth had dried and she
was sure the pulse in her temple must be audible to his ears
as well as her own. She was aware, too, of pulses in other
places, that weakened her knees and caused a hot feeling of
dampness between her legs.

'I'm—sorry,' she got out breathily. 'What did you say?'

'My mother was enquiring how you like your coffee,' he
replied, and she wondered if it was only coincidence that
made him choose that moment to run his hand over his thigh.
Whatever, she had to steel herself not to react when his clos-
est finger brushed her leg, and the impulse to grab his hand
and imprison it between her thighs was almost overpowering.

What was happening to her? With heat beading on her
upper lip, Rachel struggled to respond. 'Um—as it comes,'
she said, deciding that taking her coffee black might bring
her to her senses. 'Thank you.'

If Signora Webb was aware of the silent interchange between her son and his guest, she chose to ignore it. Instead,
she poured Rachel's coffee with an enviably steady hand before adding casually, '*Caro*, I am puzzled, no? How did
Joseph lift the wheelchair into the house? It is heavy, *e*?'

She was speaking to Gabriel, and he looked at his mother

now with cool guarded eyes. 'How do you think he did it?' he countered. 'I helped him, of course. You wouldn't have had me let Rachel do it, I am sure.'

'*Forse no*. And yet she might be better equipped to lift a heavy weight than you are,' replied his mother flatly. 'You know what the doctors have said—'

'I do not wish to discuss it now,' broke in Gabriel, clearly irritated by this unsubtle attempt to inform Rachel he wasn't a well man. He turned back to Hannah, who was drinking her Coke through a straw. 'When you've finished, we'll go and find the stables, hmm?'

'*Bene, ma fa' attenzione,* Gabriel,' exclaimed Signora Webb, offering the plate of scones to Rachel almost absently. 'I do not wish to see you in the 'ospital again.'

Rachel politely refused the scones, her mind racing with what was being said. She didn't understand all of it, but enough to confirm that Gabriel had indeed been ill. 'Um—if it's too much for you,' she began awkwardly, and Gabriel's mouth compressed.

'I've been overworking,' he told her shortly, clearly no more pleased by her enquiry than he was by his mother's. 'I've been advised to take a holiday, that is all.'

'No!' His mother was indignant. 'You had a heart attack, Gabriel,' she exclaimed fiercely, and Rachel caught her breath.

A heart attack! She was amazed at how distressed she felt at this news.

'I did not have a heart attack,' Gabriel was contradicting his mother now, and she fluttered a protesting hand.

'*Cosi buono come,*' she retorted obstinately. 'As good as. Why not be honest with yourself, *caro*? You have been told to rest, to avoid all stressful situations, to take things easy. *Perche*, you have even resigned from your job with the company.'

'I have taken leave of absence,' Gabriel corrected her, obviously getting angry, but his mother seemed indifferent to his censure.

'You see,' she said, turning to Rachel, and although Rachel would have liked to dismiss her words as scaremongering, there was genuine concern in her suddenly drawn face. 'He will not listen to me. Perhaps you can make him see sense, no?'

'Well, I—'

'Do not try and enlist Rachel's support, Mamma,' broke in Gabriel harshly. He took a deep breath before turning to Rachel again with evident strain. 'I am sorry. My mother has no right to try and involve you in our personal disagreements.'

Rachel shook her head. 'I'm sure your mother only has your best interests at heart,' she said awkwardly, and his mouth twisted.

'Are you?' he essayed grimly. 'I wish I had your optimism.' Then, getting to his feet, 'I believe you have a lunch appointment, Mamma. I expect we will meet again at supper.'

'Bene.' Signora Webb took her set-down with good grace, briefly reminding Rachel of her son. 'I am sorry if I have embarrassed you, Gabriel. But I think your guests should be aware of—of the situation.'

'What situation?' Gabriel snapped, and Rachel had never seen him so angry. 'There is no situation, Mamma. Enough! Let us hear no more about it.'

Hannah had finished her Coke now, and set the empty glass on the table. Then she looked at her mother with worried eyes. She didn't like arguments of any kind, and Rachel sometimes wondered if she remembered the rows she and Larry used to have. Whatever, any upset frightened her, particularly when she didn't understand what was going on.

'Are you all right?' Rachel began with a smile, trying to reassure her, but Gabriel had noticed the child's anxiety himself.

With what must have been a supreme effort of self-control, he forced a smile and said, 'Well, Hannah, are you ready to go exploring?'

'Yes, please.'

Hannah looked up at him with excited eyes and Rachel sighed. It was ironic, she thought, that the only man her daughter had really taken to had to be someone whose interest in them could never mean more than it did today.

'I want Mummy to come, too,' added Hannah, as Gabriel took hold of her chair, and his mouth thinned into a weary line.

'If she still wants to,' he said, his meaning obvious, and Rachel got instantly to her feet. Whatever the future might hold, she was prepared to grab the present with both hands, however foolhardy that made her.

'I'm looking forward to it,' she said, fighting the wave of wild abandon that enveloped her. And he looked so relieved she wanted to hug him. Which just proved how reckless she was.

The way to the stables was through gardens already bright with the exuberance of early summer plantings. Herbaceous borders were already overflowing with flowering plants and shrubs, and in shady corners roses and honeysuckle were budding.

There was a swimming pool, protected by a hedge of conifers, and Hannah stared at it in amazement. 'Is this all yours?' she asked, looking up at Gabriel with envious eyes, and he nodded.

'Why?' He glanced at Rachel. 'Does Hannah swim?'

'She did,' said Rachel in a low voice. And then, because he was obviously waiting for her to go on, 'Before the accident. Not since.'

'But surely water therapy—' began Gabriel at once, and then frowned as if at his own audacity. 'I'm sorry. I know nothing about it, of course.'

'No, but you're right,' conceded Rachel, with a sigh. 'Hannah's therapist was keen on the idea, but I'm afraid we only took her a couple of times.'

'Oh?' Gabriel arched an enquiring brow and Rachel was forced to continue.

'Yes.' She hesitated. She felt awkward discussing it with him. 'I—as you may or may not know, Kingsbridge doesn't have any public swimming facilities. We had to take her to the nearest town. And—well, I was at college during the day, and my mother had to take her. And as she—my mother, that is—doesn't swim—'

'I understand.' Gabriel interrupted her, his tone conciliatory. 'It was thoughtless of me to say anything. I'm sure it has been difficult for you since your husband was killed.'

Rachel stiffened. 'We manage.'

She was defensive again, and Gabriel shook his head. 'It wasn't a criticism.'

'No.' Rachel found herself giving him a rueful smile. 'I suppose I don't like talking about my personal problems either.'

'Ah.' Gabriel's dark gaze swept her face. 'You think I'm too hard on my mother?'

'I think she's concerned about you,' said Rachel, with a slight shrug of her shoulders. Then, diffidently, 'Have you been ill?'

'Do you really want to know?'

'If you want to tell me.' Rachel dipped her eyes from his disturbing gaze. 'It must have been serious if you had to give up your job.'

'It was my choice,' said Gabriel flatly. 'I didn't want to do it. Not then. But it was impossible for me to rest and remain CEO of the company.'

'Your mother said you had a heart attack,' Rachel reminded him cautiously. 'You denied it.'

'Because it wasn't a heart attack,' declared Gabriel, not without a trace of the impatience he'd shown earlier. 'Stress, yes. I'll admit to that. I hadn't been sleeping well and I was finding it hard to concentrate. I guess I'd lost some weight, too, but that's all.'

'Then why—?'

'Why has the old lady got it into her head that I had a heart attack?' Gabriel sighed. 'You can blame the medic for that. I collapsed one day at the office, and as he's an old friend of the family he offered the opinion that if I didn't take a break—'

Rachel stared at him. 'Oh, Gabriel!'

She hadn't realised she'd used his name until his face creased into a lazy smile. 'You see,' he said. 'I knew you could do it.' And, when she frowned, he added, 'Use my name. Mr Webb makes me feel even older than I already am.'

'So—so is that why you've come back here? To rest?' she asked quickly, thus avoiding his attempt to divert her. 'I'd have thought this was the last place you'd choose. With the plant just a couple of miles away. Didn't you fancy somewhere else, somewhere warmer, perhaps? Like—Italy?'

Gabriel gave her a wry look. 'I guess you've heard that I've been seeing a specialist at a hospital in Oxford,' he said cynically. 'Who told you? Your friend, Joe?'

Rachel's face flamed. 'It—it was my mother, actually. Joe has nothing to do with it.'

'Doesn't he?' Gabriel sounded sceptical. 'I'm sure he wouldn't agree with you. He was itching to tell me to keep away from you yesterday afternoon.'

Rachel gasped. 'That's ridiculous! Joe—Joe's a friend, that's all.'

'You like Joe,' said Hannah suddenly, hearing a name she recognised and distracted from trailing her fingers through the ferns that grew beside the path. 'Grandma says so.'

Grandma would, thought Rachel grimly, wishing her daughter didn't have such sharp ears. Though perhaps it was just as well that she did. She had the feeling she was getting into waters that were both deep and dangerous.

'I do like Joe,' she said now, aware that she was feeling too intense. But being with Gabriel did that to her, and the quivering in her stomach was just a manifestation of the turmoil in her head. 'I've known him a long time.'

'I don't think your liking is what he's aiming for,' remarked Gabriel softly. 'I don't blame him.'

Rachel shook her head. 'This is a pointless conversation,' she said tightly. And then, seeing an arched gateway in the distance, she took the opportunity to draw her daughter's attention to it. 'Oh, look, Hannah. I can see some horses in the paddock.'

A clematis-hung wall divided the kitchen garden from the fields and paddocks beyond. The gateway Rachel had pointed out to Hannah led into a yard flanked by white-painted stables and tack rooms, and, as well as the horses visible in the paddock, a young female groom was busy currying a chestnut mare in the stable yard. She looked up with a smile when Gabriel and his guests came into the yard, and it was obvious from her greeting that he was a welcome visitor.

'This is Katy Irving, Hannah,' Gabriel declared, bringing her chair to a halt and going round it to speak to her. 'And this mare is called Siena, which I'm sure your mother will tell you is a city in Tuscany. It's also where my mother was born.'

'Tuscany?' said Hannah doubtfully, and Rachel quickly explained.

'It's in Italy, sweetheart. That's in Europe.'

'I know where Italy is,' replied Hannah scornfully. Then, looking up at Gabriel, she added shyly, 'She's very big, isn't she?'

'But she's very friendly, too,' put in Katy before Gabriel could respond. 'I'll take you to see some of the other horses later. They're not all as big as Siena.'

'Perhaps.' Gabriel was non-committal, and Rachel was

glad he was giving the little girl time to get used to her surroundings. 'Right now, I think I'll introduce you to her foal. The one I was telling you about. He's still inside.'

'The one I'm going to choose a name for?' demanded Hannah eagerly, and Rachel marvelled again at the ease with which Gabriel won her daughter's confidence. 'Where is he?'

'I'll show you.'

Taking hold of the chair again, Gabriel wheeled Hannah across the yard, and although she glanced back once, to assure herself that her mother was following, it was obvious that she trusted him completely.

Inside the stables the air was warm and musty. The mingled scents of oats and pine disinfectant, of horses and coarse leather, were potently sensual to Rachel, and she decided she was allowing this man to have far too much of an effect on her senses. With him, she was aware of herself—of him—in a way that she'd never experienced before, and every inch of skin, every nerve in her body, responded to his sexuality.

Not that he'd actually done anything to warrant these feelings, she acknowledged tensely. Apart from expressing his attraction to her he had never laid a hand on her—not in any sexual way anyway. And she felt sure that the raw intimacy she felt in his presence must be totally self-induced.

The foal was a delight. His coat was a darker shade than his mother's, and he balanced on spindly legs that didn't seem to have strength enough to support his weight. He was shy, too, evidently unused to being separated from his mother, but, as with Hannah, Gabriel seemed to have no difficulty in persuading the foal to trust him.

'Oh!' Hannah clasped her hands together. 'Isn't he pretty!'

'He is a handsome beast,' agreed Gabriel humorously. 'Do you want to stroke him?'

'Oh, yes.'

Indeed, Hannah was desperate to get close to the foal herself, but her chair had been left at the entrance to the stall, and as Rachel watched with disbelieving eyes the little girl started to lift her feet onto the floor of the stable, as if she intended to stand up.

'I—wait—' Rachel began, certain she should intervene, but Gabriel glanced round at that moment and instantly saw what was going on.

'Hey, Hannah,' he said, his soft voice as soothing as velvet on Rachel's tender nerves, 'let me help you.' And, before anyone could object, he lifted Hannah out of the chair and into his arms. He carried her across to where the foal was waiting, nuzzling a bag of hay, and then shocked all of them by setting Hannah on her feet.

Although Rachel stepped forward almost instinctively, to stop him from letting go of the child, she needn't have worried. Gabriel had no intention of letting Hannah fall, and the little girl was so entranced by the delicate little animal that she was hardly aware of what she was doing.

With Gabriel supporting her weight, she stretched out eager hands to the foal, touching his jerking head almost reverently, smoothing her small fingers over his shining coat. 'Oh, look,' she exclaimed, as the foal turned his soft mouth into her hand. 'He likes me! He really likes me!'

'That's because you're the same size he is,' said Gabriel gently. 'You're not too big. You don't threaten him in any way.'

'Is that true?'

Hannah turned her head to look up at Gabriel again, and suddenly seemed to realise what she was doing. Rachel saw her sag against him, and once again, before she could panic, Gabriel swung her up into his arms.

'How about that?' he said, injecting an admiring note into his voice. 'You were standing and you didn't even know it.'

Hannah swallowed and looked back over her shoulder at her mother, and then, in a shaky voice, she said, 'Yes. Yes, I was, wasn't I? Did you see me, Mummy? I was standing.'

'I saw you,' said Rachel, trying not to show any of the panic she had felt when she saw what Gabriel was doing.

Trying not to feel any resentment either that her daughter should have allowed him to help her to stand when neither Rachel, her mother, nor the therapist had been able to achieve as much. She looked at him now with guarded eyes. 'But I think Mr Webb ought to put you back into your chair now.'

'Does he have to?'

Hannah was liking being in Gabriel's arms. She was so much higher than she usually was, and she could see so much more. Besides, it meant she was the centre of attention.

'I'm afraid so,' said Rachel firmly, ignoring her daughter's pursed mouth and the inward knowledge that she was being unnecessarily strict. 'I'm sure Mr Webb's doctor wouldn't approve of him carrying you around all day.'

Gabriel's mouth tightened, but he only spoke to Hannah as he set her back in the chair and adjusted the footrests. If he was annoyed with Rachel for using his illness against him again, he chose not to say so, and Katy Irving's arrival provided a welcome distraction.

'D'you want to come and see some of the other horses now?' she asked, squatting down beside the little girl's chair, and Hannah nodded enthusiastically before launching into an account of how she'd stood to stroke the foal.

'I might show you later,' she added, but Rachel couldn't have that.

'Not today,' she said firmly, aware that she was loading her fears onto the child. Then, looking at Katy, 'But I'm sure she'd love to see the horses. I'll come with you.'

'No.' Now Hannah chose to be awkward. 'I don't want you to, Mummy. I'm old enough to go on my own.'

'All right.'

Rachel couldn't help feeling a lump come into her throat at the child's words. Hannah was old enough; of course she was. Heavens, she went to her school on her own. But Rachel couldn't help the unworthy belief that it was Gabriel who had inspired this sudden bid for independence, and she didn't like it.

Katy pulled an apologetic face as she took charge of the wheelchair, and Rachel forced a smile for her benefit. 'I'll look after her, Mrs Kershaw,' Katy added, after exchanging a brief glance with her employer. 'We'll just go over to the paddocks. Okay?'

'Okay.' Rachel realised the young woman had recognised her misgivings. And that Gabriel must have told her their names in advance. Just another reason for resenting his high-handedness, she brooded. 'Bye, darling. Be good.'

'I'm always good,' muttered Hannah crossly. Then, 'G'bye, Mummy.' And this time she didn't look back as Katy wheeled her away.

However, when Rachel would have followed them out of the stables, Gabriel caught her arm. 'Wait!' He came fully out of the stall and secured the gate. 'Give them time. You don't want Hannah to think you don't trust her, do you?'

Rachel wrenched her arm out of his grasp. 'I don't think I need you to tell me what to do where Hannah is concerned,' she declared coldly. 'I suppose after that little—exhibition—' she gestured towards the stall '—you think you're the expert!'

Gabriel released her arm, but he had moved into the aisle that led out of the stables so there was no way she could beat a retreat. 'I think you're allowing your resentment towards me to blind you to the fact that I didn't actually do anything,' he retorted mildly. 'For a few moments Hannah stood on her own two feet. What's so terribly wrong with that?'

Put in such a way, Rachel found it hard to think of any objection. But she couldn't allow him to have the last word. Holding up her head, she said, 'You're building up impossible expectations in Hannah's mind.'

'Impossible?' His brows arched in speculative enquiry. 'Didn't you tell me that Hannah's paralysis was only temporary? That her doctor believes it's more psychological than physical?'

Rachel pressed her lips together before replying. 'I shouldn't have discussed Hannah's condition with you.'

'Why not?' To her dismay, he moved to narrow the gap between them. 'Are you afraid that if Hannah does get her mobility back she won't need you as much?'

'No!' Rachel was horrified. 'How dare you suggest such a thing? I want Hannah to walk again just as much as—as anyone else.'

'All right.' To her alarm, he put out his hand and tucked an errant strand of hair behind her ear. 'But it would be quite natural if you had misgivings. After all, it must have been quite a blow when you lost your husband.'

'What are you implying?' Rachel dashed his hand away. 'Do you think I'm using Hannah as a prop to boost my own self-esteem, is that it? That because Larry died I'm lacking any other purpose in my life?'

'You tell me,' he said softly, his hand falling to his side, and Rachel was suddenly incensed.

'I have no intention of telling you anything,' she stated angrily. 'Now, please, get out of my way!'

She stepped forward then, expecting him to do the decent thing and move aside, but he didn't. Instead, he remained where he was, so that her impulsive action brought her into contact with his hard unyielding body. For a moment they were chest to chest, hip to hip, and the heat of his flesh rose to meet hers. Then Rachel recoiled again, and came up painfully against the wall of the stall behind her.

Her head banged against the solid oak and for a moment she felt dizzy with the pain. She couldn't prevent the cry she emitted, but even as she lifted a hand to rub her bruised skull Gabriel forestalled her. His exclamation was much less polite than hers, and his hands came to cradle her head, pushing aside the silken weight of her hair, massaging her scalp with long probing fingers.

'Are you all right?' he demanded, his frown deepening when his fingertips found the tender spot at the back of her head and she winced. 'God, Rachel, don't you know I wouldn't hurt you? Dammit, there was no need for you to behave as if I'd attacked you.'

Rachel moved her head cautiously from side to side. 'It was my fault,' she said tightly, unhappily aware that inside she was panicking again. He was so close to her, and in the ripe humidity of the stables she couldn't help but be aware of him in a purely physical way. The collar of his shirt was open, exposing the brown column of his throat, and his scent, that clean male scent she had noticed before, was now over-laid with a trace of sweat. 'It was an accident, that was all.'

'An accident I instigated,' he said harshly, his thumbs moving to the sensitive hollows of her ears. 'I'm sorry.'

'Please...'

Rachel didn't know how much more of this she could take without betraying herself. She doubted he was aware that his thighs were against hers, that his wrists were brushing her neck, or that her anger—the anger, she realised now, she had induced to escape being alone with him—had been engulfed by other, more complicated emotions.

It would have been so easy to put up her hands and grasp his wrists. Or even to cup his dark face between her two palms and trace the sensual contours of his mouth. What would he do, she wondered, if she reached up and touched his lips with hers? If she parted her legs and drew his hand to that throbbing place between her thighs...?

'Don't look at me like that,' he said suddenly, and she realised that something of what she was feeling must be ev-ident in her face. 'For God's sake, Rachel, don't make me hate myself any more than I do already.'

'I don't know what—'

'Of course you do.' He was savage. 'You're feeling sorry for me again, aren't you? And I thought I'd explained all that. I'm not an invalid, Rachel. I'm a man. I don't want your sympathy. I want—ah, God, if you only knew.'

'Gabriel—'

She said his name softly, lingeringly, and, with a groan that mingled naked frustration with raw desire, he moved his hands to the back of her neck. He groaned again as he jerked her towards him, as his mouth searched for and found her own, but Rachel was overwhelmed by the hungry ardour of his kiss. She had never expected this, she thought incredulously, but she couldn't prevent the instinctive response that made her clutch at the neckline of his shirt and part her lips to the possessive invasion of his tongue.

Now she was glad of the barrier of the stall behind her. Without it, she was fairly sure she'd have slipped bonelessly to the floor of the stables. Maybe even taking him with her, she acknowledged dizzily, as the weight of Gabriel's hard body pressed sensuously against hers. God, what was she thinking? There were grooms and other stable hands around. Did she want the world and his wife to know that she wanted this man to—to—?

To what?

His hands had moved from her nape to the collar of her shirt, his fingers probing the hollows of her throat as his tongue probed the moist recesses of her mouth. Beneath the thin fabric her breasts felt tight and swollen, and she didn't object when he wedged one leg between her trembling thighs. Indeed, she was glad of the support, although she was half afraid the hot wetness she could feel there would communicate itself to him.

But that awareness alone was enough to convince her that she was only fooling herself in pretending she didn't know what she wanted from this man. Crazy as it seemed—crazy as it undoubtedly was—she wanted him to make love with her. Here, now, on the stable floor if that was what he wanted. She didn't care. She just knew she was aching for him to do it.

'God, Rachel!'

His strangled use of her name was sobering. That, and the realisation that he was trembling, too. Although his mouth was still delivering burning, urgent kisses over every inch of her face, his fingers were now biting into the bones of her shoulders. She had the feeling he was as fiercely angry with her now as he had been with his mother earlier, and she swallowed her chagrin when he abruptly thrust himself back from her yielding body.

'We can't do this.'

'No.'

How Rachel got the denial out she never knew, but somehow she managed to articulate the word. And to gather her scattered senses. At least to the extent that she was able to stiffen her legs and draw herself up against the wall behind her with an element of dignity. But inside she was in turmoil, and she didn't know how she was going to get through the remainder of the visit pretending that what happened had meant as little to her as it had apparently meant to him.

'This wasn't meant to happen,' he continued, raking hands that shook a little through his dark hair. Hair that was damp along his hairline, Rachel noticed, not sure whether that was a good sign or a bad one. 'God, you're going to think I had this in mind all along.'

'And you didn't?'

Rachel didn't know why she'd said those words, unless perhaps she'd sensed that he wasn't quite telling the truth here. And although she'd spoken barely audibly he heard her, and a look that mixed anger and self-contempt in equal measures spread over his lean, harsh face.

'All right,' he conceded after a moment. 'Of course I've thought about it, about how you'd react if I touched you. If I'm totally honest I'll admit I've thought of little else since— well, since I got to know you, I suppose. But I was fairly sure you'd never agree to go out with me, so I was able to keep my baser instincts under control.' He lips twisted. 'Pathetic, huh?'

Rachel bent her head. 'I wouldn't say that,' she ventured softly. 'Not unless you're sorry you touched me.'

Gabriel stared at her. 'What's that supposed to mean? I've just told you how I feel.'

'No, you haven't.' Rachel lifted her head to look at him. 'All you've done is berate yourself for giving in to something that—well, that seems perfectly natural to me.'

'Yeah, right.' Patently he didn't believe her. 'Any minute now you're going to tell me you understand why I did it. Why I behaved like a—like a sex-starved savage the minute I got you alone.'

Rachel shook her head. 'You didn't behave like a sex-starved savage,' she protested. 'You—kissed me, that's all.' She hesitated. 'It was no big deal.'

'Really?' Gabriel's expression had darkened now. 'Does that mean you're in the habit of letting men put their hands all over you? That you don't see anything wrong in the fact that I practically tried to seduce you?'

'Of course not—'

Rachel was horrified, but Gabriel didn't give her a chance to explain that she had been trying to reassure him. 'I'm obviously behind the times,' he said harshly. 'I'd forgotten that women today pride themselves on being equal to men. In every way.'

'I'm not like that,' Rachel gasped, but he wasn't listening to her.

'I guess this is the way Andrew treated you, right?' His lips curled. 'Perhaps I should have taken some advice from my son before embarking on such a perilous course. I'm sure he wouldn't have attempted to apologise for something that was—*no big deal*!'

'Oh, Gabriel!' Rachel closed her eyes against the pain in his. 'Don't do this! What happened between us has nothing to do with Andrew. Not as far as I'm concerned, anyway.'

Gabriel was bitter. 'You expect me to believe that?'

Rachel felt suddenly weary. 'I don't expect anything from you,' she replied, opening her eyes again and drawing herself up to her full height. 'I don't even understand you. I particularly don't understand what you want me to say. But, just for the record, I never went to bed with your son, whatever he may have told you. Now, if you'll step out of my way...'

Gabriel groaned. 'God, Rachel—'

'I mean it,' she said, almost at the end of her strength. 'I want to go and find my daughter.'

'Not yet.' Gabriel looked exhausted himself, deep lines etched beside his mouth—the mouth that only moments before had been giving her so much pleasure. 'We have to talk—'

But he never finished what he was going to say. As he stepped forward to detain her, a bucket clattered behind them. One of the stable hands had come into the building to water the animals and he waved cheerfully at his employer.

'Not disturbing you, am I, sir?' he asked, and Gabriel was forced to move away from Rachel to speak to him.

It was the chance she needed. Dragging the sides of her jacket across her chest, because she wasn't absolutely sure all the buttons on her shirt were fastened, she walked swiftly along the aisle and out of the stables. If the man who'd disturbed them was surprised at her exit, he knew better than to show it, and Rachel stood outside in the paved yard, dragging the bracing air into her starved lungs.

CHAPTER EIGHT

IT TOOK an enormous effort of will for Rachel to get out of bed on Monday morning. When the alarm went off at a quarter to seven she would have liked nothing better than to ignore it and bury her head in the pillow again. She didn't want to get up. She didn't want to face the day. And what she most especially didn't want to think about was what had happened between her and Gabriel the day before.

The sound of her mother moving around in the bathroom next door proved a powerful stimulant, however. If Mrs Redfern so much as suspected that their outing to Copleys had not been a total success, Rachel would never hear the end of it, and she simply couldn't cope with that today. So far, she had managed to distract Mrs Redfern with the news that Hannah had actually stood on her own two feet for a few moments and, although her mother obviously had reservations—as Rachel had herself—the older woman had made the little girl feel proud of the achievement. And as far as Hannah was concerned they had had a good time, and that was the way Rachel wanted it to stay.

And Hannah had, admitted Rachel reluctantly. The little girl had been in her element, feeding lumps of sugar to the horses and enjoying the unusual position of being the centre of attraction. Certainly the groom and stable hands had all made a fuss of her, and she had loved it. For the first time since the accident Rachel had seen her daughter as she'd used to be: relaxed and happy, and brimming with confidence.

The hard part to swallow was that it was all due to Gabriel's kindness. It was he who had arranged the visit, he who had instigated that nerve-racking moment when she'd stood alone, he who had given the child the male attention she had spurned for so long. Not for the first time Rachel was obliged to acknowledge his patience where her daughter was concerned.

She had been a little anxious after that embarrassing scene in the stables that he might take his frustrations out on the little girl. But she should have known better. Whatever he thought of her, whatever misplaced impression she had given him regarding her experience with men, his attitude towards Hannah hadn't changed. Indeed, if anything, he had been even more attentive to her, as if to prove to Rachel that, however she behaved, he was nothing like his son.

As if she had ever imagined that he was.

Hannah was talkative at breakfast. Rachel had thought the little girl had said everything there was to say the night before, but evidently she was wrong. Hannah had been tired last night and although she'd talked non-stop all through supper, about how she'd felt when Gabriel had let her stand to stroke the foal, and how she was still thinking about what Gabriel should call it, she had fallen asleep soon after. But today, with rather less discretion, she started telling her grandmother about the row Gabriel had had with his mother before they'd gone out to feed the horses, and Rachel wanted to groan at the sudden gleam in her mother's eyes.

'It wasn't a row,' she protested, giving the child a reproving stare. 'Eat your cornflakes, Hannah. You're going to be late.'

'She's got plenty of time,' remarked Mrs Redfern smugly. 'It's you who's going to be late, Rachel. If you don't hurry up, you won't have any coffee made before you open up.'

'Anyway, it was a row,' continued Hannah, undeterred. She looked at her grandmother with wide assertive eyes. 'Gabe's mother said he'd had a heart attack,' she added proudly. 'And he said he hadn't.'

'A heart attack,' murmured Mrs Redfern consideringly. 'Hmm, so that's what's brought him back to Copleys. I knew it must be something serious.'

'It wasn't a heart attack,' stated Rachel irritably, getting up from the table. 'So don't go telling people it was. He— well, he'd been overworking and he's been advised to rest. That's all.'

'So you say.'

'So I know,' snapped Rachel curtly. Then, she fixed her daughter with a cold look. 'And I'd have thought that after all the attention Gabriel paid to you yesterday, you'd know better than to start gossiping about him.'

Hannah's lower lip trembled. 'I wasn't gossiping.'

'Of course you were.' But Rachel didn't really have the time to cope with Hannah's tears now. 'Anyway, just remember what I've said. You weren't even supposed to be listening to that conversation.'

'And how's the child supposed to close her ears to other people's conversation?' demanded Mrs Redfern shortly, and Rachel decided, somewhat uncharitably, that her mother was afraid she was going to lose out here. She'd switched off when Hannah was telling her about the horses last night, Rachel had noticed, but any titbits about the Webbs were infinitely more appealing.

'Well, Hannah knows how I feel about it,' Rachel added, collecting her jacket and bag from the hall. 'I'll see you two later, okay?' She bent to kiss her daughter's soft cheek. 'Have a good day.'

The bus she sometimes caught passed the end of the road before she got there. Which was par for the course, she thought wearily, realising she would have to walk to work. She had hoped to avoid having any more time for introspection, but the memory of what had happened yesterday just kept intruding.

Not that anything more humiliating had happened after that heated exchange in the stables. For the rest of the time they were there Hannah had been with them, and her excited chatter had filled any awkward gaps there might have been.

She'd wanted to know if she could come again and ride

one of the horses. And, although Rachel had been firmly convinced that they would not be coming here again, for any reason, she had let Gabriel explain that Hannah would need a special saddle before she could sit on a horse herself.

Of course, he'd gone on to offer to try and borrow one from the local riding stables, but Rachel had demurred. Riding was not something Hannah had been advised to try, and in any case, she'd added, looking at the child and not at him, children rode ponies, not full-sized horses. The subject had been dropped, much to Hannah's disappointment, and Rachel had justified her position by reminding herself that riding lessons were out of their league anyway.

Lunch had been a strained meal. For Rachel, at least. It should have been easier, with his mother absent and just the three of them at the informal table in the morning room, but it hadn't been. Apart from her own antipathy towards Gabriel, there had been the added unfamiliarity of being served by strangers, all of whom must have wondered what their employer was doing with a woman whose only claim to fame was the fact that she ran the local coffee shop.

Gabriel himself hadn't seemed at all concerned, of course. However angry he'd been with her in the stables, he'd evidently succeeded in getting his feelings under control and had even conversed with her throughout the meal, albeit about inconsequential, impersonal things like the weather. Certainly he'd succeeded in convincing Hannah that there was nothing amiss, and for that Rachel supposed she should be grateful. After all, she could imagine how morbidly curious her mother would have been if Hannah had announced that she and Gabriel had stopped speaking to one another.

They'd left immediately after lunch, much to Hannah's disappointment. Rachel had guessed her daughter had hoped to pay a return visit to the stables before they left, but as far as she'd been concerned that was completely out of the question. However, she'd not been unaware of the cynically sceptical look Gabriel had given her when she'd professed to having a mountain of paperwork awaiting her back home. If she'd thought she could fool him, she'd been mistaken.

But what of it? she chided herself now, quickening her step. It wasn't as if she was likely to see him again. Or wanted to, she appended grimly. She wasn't altogether sure he was that different from Andrew, after all. Not when it came to having respect for her, at least.

The day went from bad to worse. As her mother had predicted, some of her early customers arrived before she'd had the coffee started. And, later on, when she'd tried to turn on the oven Joe had repaired for her the previous week, it refused to work.

Stephanie arrived to find her employer struggling to cope with just one oven and, although it was of commercial size, it certainly couldn't handle all the pasta dishes they usually sold at midday. Rachel's lasagne was popular with the lunch-time crowd and having to disappoint her customers was not good business.

'Have you tried to reach Joe?' Stephanie asked, making her own inspection of the oven and finding it stone-cold. 'Maybe he could do something on a temporary basis, at least.'

'The last time he repaired it he said I needed a new oven,' replied Rachel, unwilling to admit that she had her own reasons for not wanting to contact Joe today. 'It's so old, he can't get the spares any more.'

'Even so...'

'I'm going to have to change the menu, that's all,' said Rachel flatly. 'We'll concentrate on soups and salads today and hope that no one asks for anything else. We can always use the microwave in an emergency.'

Stephanie regarded her consideringly. 'So are you going to ring Joe or not?'

'Not right now, no,' said Rachel, keeping her eyes averted. 'Oh, here's Patsy. I was beginning to think she wasn't coming.'

'It is only half-past nine,' pointed out Stephanie drily, donning her apron. 'Are you going to tell me the real reason why you're not getting in touch with Joe? Let me guess: he came on to you at the craft fair on Saturday and you blew him out.'

'How did you know he was at the craft fair on Saturday?' demanded Rachel, before she could stop herself, and Stephanie smirked.

'Wasn't everyone? Even Gabriel Webb was there, as you know.' She paused, her eyes narrowing a little speculatively. 'Did he stay here long after I went home?'

'Joe?' Rachel chose to be obtuse. 'He didn't come in to the café on Saturday at all. He didn't come on to me at the craft fair. And I didn't blow him out, so there.'

'We were talking about Gabriel Webb,' said Stephanie doggedly. 'Are you seeing him again?'

'Not as far as I know.'

Rachel turned away to greet her younger employee, but Stephanie wasn't finished. 'So, why not? What happened? He seemed pretty interested to me.'

'What is this? An inquisition?' Rachel knew that sooner or later Stephanie was bound to find out about her visit to Copleys, but not yet. 'We had tea together, right? Hannah likes him. Now, can we get back to what we're going to serve for lunch?'

'What's wrong?' Patsy wanted to know, and Rachel was glad to tell her about the oven. It gave her a breathing space, and she was distracted from her own worries when the girl offered to go to the bakers and get some French bread.

'You could offer people a ploughman's lunch as one alternative,' she suggested, and Rachel gave her an approving smile.

'So we could,' she applauded. And then, to Stephanie, 'You should be thinking up ideas like this instead of wasting time asking questions. And Joe Collins isn't necessarily the answer. But I will ask his advice later. There's nothing he can do while the café's open, is there?'

'I guess not.' Stephanie shrugged. 'Okay. What kind of soup are we going to offer?'

Despite Rachel's show of optimism, her lunchtime customers weren't best pleased to find the menu had changed. And, although she assured them it was only temporary, she didn't honestly see how she was going to afford a new oven, second-hand or otherwise. Besides, despite what she'd told Stephanie, she wasn't at all convinced that Joe would forgive her for the way she'd treated him on Saturday. And without his help things looked very black indeed.

Then, at half-past one, when most of the lunchtime crowd had left to go back to work, Gabriel walked into the café.

Patsy saw him first, and she came hurrying across to where Rachel was stacking plates to say, 'That man's here again,' in a stage whisper.

'What man?' Stephanie swung round and saw their visitor and her eyes gleamed with mischief. 'Hey, Rachel, let's hope he hasn't come to try your famous lasagne.'

Rachel stifled a groan. What was *he* doing here? After the way she'd left Copleys the previous afternoon, she'd felt sure she was never likely to see him again.

Yet here he was, as dark and inscrutable as when she'd first seen him, his charcoal-grey trousers and black jacket deepening the sallow cast of his lean features. He didn't look well, was her first thought, and the second was, why should she care?

'Oh-oh, he's coming over,' added Stephanie, clearly seeing this as the high point of their day. 'Do you want to serve him, or shall we let Patsy do the honours? I'd have thought he'd have realised this isn't a self-service café by now.'

Rachel pressed her lips together. 'I'll do it,' she said, not at all convinced that Gabriel had come into the café to be served. And if he hadn't... A shiver ran down her spine. What else could he want? Surely he didn't intend to embarrass her by saying what he hadn't been able to say in Hannah's presence here?

He reached the counter, hands pushed into the pockets of his jacket, shoulders hunched even though it was a warm early summer day outside. And, however Stephanie viewed his arrival, she had the sense to withdraw into the kitchen as Patsy busied herself by going to clear the rest of the tables.

Rachel was intensely conscious of her appearance. The upheaval the defunct oven had caused had left high colour in her cheeks, and her hair, which she had skewered on top of her head with hairpins borrowed from Stephanie, was damp around the edges. Her apron, too, was splashed with the soup she had made earlier, and despite his drawn features she was very aware of the obvious gulf between them.

Forcing a tight smile—the kind of smile she reserved for awkward customers—she approached the counter. 'Tea?' she asked, her voice cool and controlled, and he pulled a wry face.

'Thank you, but no,' he responded, his eyes far too intent on her flushed face. 'What's wrong?'

'I don't know what you mean.' Rachel squared her shoulders. 'What could be wrong with asking if you wanted tea? That's why you usually come in here, isn't it?'

'That wasn't what I meant and you know it.' Gabriel regarded her curiously. 'Something's happened. I can't believe my coming in here is responsible for that look of anxiety on your face.'

'You're imagining things.' Rachel refused to let him disconcert her. 'Now, can we move on?'

'Okay.' Gabriel's mouth compressed. 'If that's the way you want to play it.'

'I'm not playing.' Rachel knew she was being unnecessarily rude but she couldn't help it. After the morning she had had she didn't need this kind of aggravation, particularly as he was partly responsible for the way she was feeling. 'Do you want serving or don't you?'

'I didn't come in here to be served,' he replied flatly. 'Well, not in any way you're likely to agree to.' His lips twisted with deliberate mockery. 'I need to talk to you.'

'No, you don't.' Rachel spoke in a low voice, glancing a little awkwardly behind her. 'We said all there was to say yesterday.'

'Why do women always talk in clichés?' he demanded wearily. 'We said nothing yesterday and you know it.'

'I don't know any such thing.'

'Then you should.' He exhaled heavily. 'I suppose you're going to hold what I said about you and Andrew against me, aren't you? Well, believe me, you can't regret it any more than I do myself.'

'Is that intended to reassure me?'

'No. It's a very poor attempt to explain that people sometimes say things in stressful situations that they don't necessarily mean,' he retorted grimly. 'Dammit, Rachel, I'm out of practice when it comes to dealing with women—any women—let alone a much younger woman like you.'

'Oh, right.' Rachel was scornful. 'You'll be telling me next that there haven't been any women since your wife died, and that was—what? Ten years ago?'

'Twelve,' he corrected her shortly. Then, taking one hand out of his pocket, he raked his nails across his scalp. 'And, of course, I'm not trying to tell you that. There have been women since Celeste died. I don't deny it. I'm not a monk!'

'There you are, then!'

Rachel was triumphant and Gabriel scowled. 'The difference is that I didn't care what they thought of me,' he said harshly. Then, glancing impatiently around the almost empty café, he took a deep breath. 'God!' A cynical smile hovered at the corners of his mouth. 'I must be crazy coming here, expecting you to listen to me now.' He turned away. 'I'll go. Maybe I'll have better luck later.'

And maybe he wouldn't, thought Rachel unhappily, as he walked swiftly across the floor and out of the café. Maybe he wouldn't even try. And who could blame him? She hadn't exactly tried to understand what he was saying.

'What was all that about?'

As usual, Stephanie wanted to know what was going on, and Rachel sighed. 'Nothing,' she said, refusing to get into yet another discussion of Gabriel's intentions. 'I think I might phone Joe now. Perhaps he'll be able to come and have a look at the oven this afternoon, after we close.'

Stephanie's arched brows were telling, but she refrained from saying anything else. It was enough that whatever Gabriel had said had apparently persuaded Rachel to speak to Joe Collins. After all, all their futures depended on the café continuing to function as normal.

Joe turned up about five o'clock. He had exhibited no animosity when Rachel had rung him on his mobile to tell him what had happened, and she tried not to feel guilty that she depended on his manual skills so much.

She had hoped Stephanie might hang around to find out whether the oven was able to be repaired for herself, but she'd said she had shopping to do and left with Patsy at a quarter to five. Consequently, Rachel was alone when Joe arrived, and she wondered if he was thinking of the way they had parted on Saturday afternoon as she was.

'Thanks for coming so promptly,' she said, deciding to try and keep their conversation on an impersonal level. 'It looks like I'm going to have to get another oven, as you said.'

'We'll see,' said Joe non-committally, setting his toolbox down and regarding the faulty oven with considering eyes. 'What happened?'

'It just refused to work this morning,' replied Rachel, propping her hip against the counter. 'I had to change the lunch-time menu. I needed the other oven for scones and pastries.'

'Mmm.'

Joe bent and rummaged in his toolbox for a screwdriver and began attacking the controls, and Rachel straightened and took a deep breath. 'Would you like a coffee?'

'No, thanks.' Joe shook his head. 'But a cold drink wouldn't come amiss. I bet it's eighty degrees outside.'

'Is it?' Rachel hadn't realised it was so hot. She'd imagined her rise in temperature was due to circumstances, but now she felt relieved. 'How about a Coke? That's Hannah's favourite.'

'Sounds good to me.'

Joe didn't look at her as he spoke and Rachel went to take a bottle from the fridge. Perhaps he had taken the hint, she thought, hoping it was so. She didn't want to fall out with him. He'd been enormously helpful since she opened the café, keeping the electrical appliances in good working order, arranging for her to have a dishwasher plumbed into the kitchen. But she had paid him for his services, she defended herself firmly. She hadn't asked for any handouts.

'How does it look?' she enquired a few minutes later when he paused to take a drink from the bottle of Coke she had set beside him. 'Is it bad?'

'It's not good,' conceded Joe, regarding her with cool appraising eyes. 'I'd say you definitely need a replacement.'

'Oh, Lord!' It was what she had feared he was going to say and the grain of hope she'd kept alive flickered and died. 'So what do I do now?'

She hadn't really been talking to him. She'd posed the question to herself as she struggled to come to terms with the bad news. But Joe chose to take it personally, and he crossed his arms over his midriff and said, 'Do you want me to help you?'

Rachel hesitated. 'You mean, with one of the ovens from Chadwick's Bakery?' she asked cautiously, and Joe gave her a considering stare.

'There is another alternative,' he said, and Rachel gazed at him with enquiring eyes. 'I've got a bit of money put by,' he went on. 'I might be persuaded to invest it with you. Both these ovens are old. The whole place needs a makeover.'

Rachel could hardly hide her astonishment. 'You mean,

you'd be prepared to lend me the money to renovate the kitchens?' She shook her head. 'Oh, Joe, that's really kind of you, but I couldn't afford to pay off another loan. If the bank would increase my overdraft, I might—'

'Who said anything about a loan?' he interrupted her. 'I'm talking about a partnership, Rachel. You need money; I've got it. What could be simpler?'

'Oh, no.' Rachel spoke hurriedly, before he could imagine she was thinking about it. 'That is...' She didn't want to offend him, but how else could she tell him that there was no way she'd consider going into partnership with him? 'It's very good of you to offer, Joe, but—well, this is my business. I want to keep it that way.'

'So what's your solution?'

He was belligerent now, and she wondered if this day could possibly get any worse.

'I don't know,' she said, hoping to reason with him. 'I mean, if you could let me have one of those ovens you're dismantling, I might be able to persuade Mr Lawrence that it would be worth his while to support me. After all, the bank isn't going to get the money I already owe them if I go out of business, are they?' she added, with a forced laugh.

'I may have another buyer for the ovens I'm taking out of Chadwick's,' responded Joe shortly. 'The last time we talked about it you said it would cause too much upset to pull the old oven out.'

'That was before—'

She had been going to say before the oven broke down again, but Joe second-guessed her. 'Before old man Webb started taking an interest in you,' he accused. 'I know. I saw him follow you out of the church hall on Saturday.'

Rachel's jaw dropped. 'I was going to say, that was before I found myself in this mess,' she contradicted him hotly. 'And I don't think my friendship with Mr Webb has anything to do with you.'

'Friendship? Is that what you call it?' Joe was scathing.

'Don't you have the sense to realise that what he really wants is a taste of whatever it was his son got from you?'

Rachel gasped. 'How dare you?'

'I dare because I care about you,' retorted Joe, red-faced himself now. 'Dammit, Rachel, I don't want to hurt you, but you don't honestly think it's your scintillating conversation he's after, do you?'

Rachel felt sick. 'What do you think he's after, Joe?' she asked unsteadily. 'I'd like to know.'

'You do know,' he muttered, putting down the Coke he had been cradling against his hip and coming towards her. 'Oh, Rachel, he wants to get into your bed, of course. Or get you into his.' His hands closed on her stiff shoulders and he gave her a cajoling shake. 'You know I'm right.'

'Get your hands off me!'

Rachel couldn't bear to have him touch her, and she would have jerked away. But he wouldn't let her. His hands clung tenaciously to her upper arms, and although she turned her head aside, he bent and tried to fasten his mouth to hers.

'Come on, Rachel,' he whispered, his wet mouth against her hot cheek. 'You know you want this just as much as I do.'

CHAPTER NINE

'I REALLY don't think she does.'

The cool sardonic tones were marvellously familiar, and Rachel managed to twist her head round far enough to see Gabriel standing just inside the café doorway, his shoulder propped against the jamb.

Joe had heard him, too, and recognised the mocking note in Gabriel's voice, and now he swung round, his face assuming an ugly belligerence. 'Who asked your opinion?' he snarled. 'And what are you doing here anyway? I'm pretty sure Rachel wouldn't have invited me if she'd known you were coming.'

Gabriel straightened away from the door. He had changed his clothes since that morning, Rachel noticed. Now he was wearing a dark grey suit in fine wool that, despite its obvious designer label, hung on his leaner frame. And, although he had spoken confidently enough, his features now drew together in a frown.

'Did you invite him, Rachel?' he asked, arching a dark brow, and Rachel gave a weary nod of her head.

'Yes, but—'

'So that's all you need to know, pal,' broke in Joe, stepping round the counter in a decidedly threatening manner. 'Rachel doesn't need you. She has plenty of friends to look after her interests. Friends who don't expect favours for helping her out.'

'Like you, you mean?'

To Rachel's consternation, Gabriel seemed undeterred by the other man's aggression, and Joe bristled now with indignation.

'What's that supposed to mean?'

'I should have thought it was fairly obvious,' drawled Gabriel, taking a deliberate step forward. 'What favours were you expecting for—what was it you said?—helping Rachel out?'

'Why, you—'

Joe would have tried to grab the lapels of Gabriel's jacket then if Rachel hadn't flown round the counter and grasped his arm.

'Are you crazy?' she demanded, and Joe turned to give her an angry look.

'What? Are you defending him?' he exclaimed, trying to shake her off as he would a worrying puppy. 'He insulted me. I don't let anyone insult me. Least of all jerks like him. Not even to please you.'

'And what are you going to do about it?' cried Rachel impatiently. 'Hit him? Beat him up?' Her eyes flicked briefly to Gabriel's cool indifferent face. 'I can just see the headlines now: "Business Tycoon Attacked by Local Man. Joe Collins, whose electrical repair company depends on commercial support, up in court for striking an influential member of the business community." Yeah, right. Go ahead and destroy your future, why don't you?'

Joe wrenched his arm away from her now, but he didn't make any move towards Gabriel. Instead, he moved back to lounge against the counter behind him, arms extended at either side as if to show that, although he'd thought better of attacking anyone, he was still in control.

'Rachel's right,' he said scornfully. 'I don't have half the town council in my pocket. Why should I risk losing my business for a creep like you?'

Gabriel rocked back on his heels. 'I still think you should leave,' he said steadily. 'Unless Rachel was just putting on a show for my benefit.'

Rachel's face burned. 'Joe came to look at one of the ovens,' she said, ignoring the younger man's attempt to silence her. 'He—he'd just told me I needed a new oven before you arrived.'

'And he was—what? Comforting you?' enquired Gabriel dispassionately, and Rachel wanted to hit him now.

'No,' she said sharply. 'He—' She turned to look at Joe and then away again. 'He was just leaving.'

'Rachel!' Joe straightened, the flush he had acquired earlier deepening to an unhealthy puce. 'For God's sake, Rachel, you don't really want me to leave, do you?' And when she didn't answer he added, 'If I go, I won't be coming back.'

'I'm sorry, Joe,' she said, turning away, and with a muttered oath he went to collect his toolbox before striding angrily out of the café.

Gabriel stepped aside as he stormed past, but Joe didn't even look at him. Rachel was sure he blamed her for what had happened even more than he blamed Gabriel, and she dreaded to think what her mother would say when she heard about this.

The door slammed behind him and for a few moments there was an uneasy silence in the room. And then Rachel gathered herself together sufficiently to round the counter again and stare in some consternation at the mess Joe had left. He had dismantled the controls of the oven before deciding there was nothing he could do and he'd left all the bits and pieces, the screws and switches and strips of metal, all over the floor.

'This is the faulty oven, I presume?'

She had been unaware that Gabriel had come to stand beside her until he spoke. 'I—yes,' she answered unwillingly, hoping he didn't think she wanted any help from him. 'I'm going to have to find another electrician.'

'I thought you said Collins told you it was beyond repair?'

'Well, he did.' Rachel hesitated. 'But I suppose I ought to get a second opinion, anyway.'

'Why?' Gabriel looked down at her with dark hooded eyes. 'Because you suspect he might have had another agenda?

One that included a certain amount of—what shall we call it? Give and take?'

Rachel's hand lashed out before she could stop it, but, whatever else was wrong with him, Gabriel's reflexes responded with admirable speed. Almost unhurriedly, it seemed, he caught Rachel's wrist on its upward trajectory, preventing the slap she'd wanted to deliver from connecting with his face. 'I don't think so, do you?' he asked softly. 'You may think I'm a poor excuse for a man, but I draw the line at being assaulted for asking what seems to me to be a perfectly reasonable question.'

Rachel clenched her teeth to prevent her jaw from trembling. 'Reasonable?' she got out, wondering if he realised how close to breaking down she was. 'You were implying I was letting Joe—letting him take advantage of me because of—because I needed his help.'

'Hardly.' Gabriel released her wrist and expelled a weary sigh. 'As a matter of fact, I was agreeing with you. I think you should have another electrician take a look at the oven.'

Rachel rubbed her wrist to restore the circulation and expelled a weary sigh. 'If you say so,' she muttered, feeling an idiot for accusing him. 'I'll look in *Yellow Pages*.'

Gabriel hesitated. 'Perhaps you'd let me help you?'

'No, thanks.'

Rachel was already rummaging under the counter for the telephone directory and he shook his head. 'Don't blame me for your friend Joe's indiscretions, Rachel,' he said flatly. 'He wasn't exactly listening to reason when I walked in.'

'I know.'

'So what's wrong with me helping you find an alternative tradesman?' His lips twisted. 'I promise I won't jump you if you say yes.'

Rachel permitted herself a covert look at his dark face. 'You don't have to help me.'

'Dammit, I know that.' Gabriel swore then. 'For God's sake, I have a staff of—I don't know—maybe a dozen or more electricians working at the Kingsbridge plant. Why shouldn't I ask one of them to come and give you their opinion of the oven?'

Rachel hesitated. 'Do you think one them would be willing to—?' She broke off. 'Of course they would. You pay their wages.'

'The company does,' he amended drily. 'But, yes, I think I can promise you there'd be no objection.'

'And do you think they'll know anything about ovens like these?'

'Some of them must do,' declared Gabriel. 'There are ovens in the canteen at the plant. I imagine they're fairly familiar with their mechanics.'

Rachel straightened. 'All right.' She licked her dry lips. 'Thank you.'

Gabriel breathed deeply for a moment and then produced a mobile phone from his pocket. He punched out a number and in a few short words he explained the position to someone at the plant. Probably the manager, thought Rachel wryly, as he put the phone away again. Someone had assured him that one of the employees would drop everything to come and examine an oven that had absolutely no connection to Webb's Pharmaceuticals.

'One of the men will be here in about—' he glanced at his watch '—in about twenty minutes. Can you hang on that long?'

'Of course.' Rachel cast an embarrassed look about her. 'Thanks. I appreciate it.'

'No worries.' Gabriel was dismissive. 'Do you want me to go?'

Rachel looked up at him. 'I—that's your decision.'

'Is it?' His mouth turned down. 'I just don't want you to get the idea that I have some hope of taking up where Collins left off.'

'I don't think that.' Rachel made a helpless gesture. 'Um—can I get you something, then? A cup of tea? Coffee?'

'Why don't we go across the road and I'll buy something to calm you down?' Gabriel suggested mildly. 'You can leave a note on the door telling the electrician where you are.'

'Oh, but—' Rachel indicated the mess of screws and metal on the floor. 'I thought I might clear this up.'

'Why?' Gabriel lifted his shoulders. 'It's going to have to be dismantled again, isn't it? Leave it. You look—shattered.'

Rachel felt shattered, but she sensed he meant something different from the way she felt. Her apron was smudged with oil now, and the hair at her temples was damp with sweat. She needed a shower and a change of clothes, and he probably would regret making the offer if she took him up on it.

'I look a mess,' she murmured, giving him the chance to pull out if he wanted to, and he gave a resigned sigh.

'You don't want to go for a drink?'

'I didn't say that.'

'Okay.' He gestured towards the door. 'Then let's go before the electrician arrives and you decide you need to stay and supervise him instead.'

Rachel shook her head, but she obediently pulled off her apron and cast a rueful glance down at her cream shirt and chocolate-brown shorts. Well, they were creased but they were clean, she consoled herself wryly. Even if they weren't in the same league as Gabriel's suit.

The bar of the Golden Lion was busier this afternoon. Tourists filled many of the booths and she and Gabriel were forced to take two stools at the bar. It meant they'd have little chance for private conversation, she thought, but that was probably just as well. Just because he'd come back she shouldn't start wondering if he'd meant what he said at lunchtime.

'What can I get you, Mr Webb?' The barman had recognised Gabriel and this time he noticed Rachel as well. 'Nice to see you, too, Mrs Kershaw,' he added, with a friendly grin, but Rachel cringed at the thought of how their association might be construed among his regulars.

'I'll have a beer, Jack,' Gabriel replied, glancing her way. 'And Mrs Kershaw will have a gin and tonic, thanks.'

'Coming up.'

The barman turned away to attend to their order and Rachel stared impatiently at the man beside her. 'A gin and tonic?' she echoed, her expression mirroring her dismay. 'I drink orange juice, or had you forgotten?'

'You drank wine at lunch yesterday,' he reminded her coolly. 'Besides, you need the alcohol. Trust me.'

Rachel rested one elbow on the bar. 'Do I have to remind you that I have a six-year-old waiting for me at home? What's she going to think if I come in smelling of alcohol?'

'Buy a pack of peppermints,' said Gabriel carelessly. 'One gin and tonic is not going to make that much difference.'

'To you, maybe,' retorted Rachel, fuelling her anger in a deliberate attempt to dispel the intimacy she felt in his presence. 'Well, don't expect me to drink it, that's all.'

'Why don't you chill out?' suggested Gabriel in a low voice, and before she could guess what he was about to do he leant towards her and deposited a warm kiss at the corner of her mouth. 'Relax. You've had a rough day, that's all.'

Rachel stared at him. 'Do you think—that—makes it any easier?' she demanded, furious that he should choose to kiss her in front of all these people. 'My God, anyone could have seen you!'

'So what?' He was uncaring. 'I've got nothing to hide.'

'You don't mean that.'

'Of course I mean it.' His eyes searched her face, lingering longest on her mouth. 'Does that make me as bad as Collins in your eyes?'

'Actually it was what he said,' she said shortly, hating herself for wanting to deny it, and he frowned.

'Collins? He said I was as bad as he was?'

'No.' Rachel heaved an exasperated sigh. 'He said—oh, it

doesn't matter what he said. I don't want to think about him at all.'

'I do.' Their drinks were brought, and after a swift word to the barman Gabriel pushed her glass towards her. 'Tell me. I'd like to hear what he thinks about me.'

'And you'll do what? Report him to the Chamber of Trade?'

Gabriel gave her a retiring look. 'I don't do things like that. Contrary to what you think, I can fight my own battles when I have to.'

Rachel didn't doubt it. He was no coward. Despite Joe's aggression, Gabriel hadn't backed down.

'So?' he persisted now, and, half-unthinking, she lifted her glass to her lips.

As he had intimated, the unfamiliar spirit was instantly reviving and she licked a pearl of tonic from her lips before proceeding. 'He—he seems to think you have designs on my body,' she said, amazed at her own temerity, and Gabriel's mouth curled in a lazy smile.

'He must be sharper than I thought,' he remarked, taking a drink of his beer. 'Chalk one up to Mr Collins!'

Rachel shivered in spite of the heat of the bar. 'That's not funny.'

'It wasn't meant to be funny.' Gabriel turned towards her, his eyes disturbingly intent. 'I've never denied it. And after the way I behaved yesterday I'm surprised you have any doubts.'

Rachel stiffened. 'So what Joe said was true? You do want to sleep with me?'

Gabriel put out his hand and wiped a smudge of moisture from her lip with his thumb. 'There's no harm in wishing, is there?'

Rachel's breathing quickened. 'I don't believe this.'

'Why not?' Gabriel's lips twisted. 'Because you can't imagine us in bed together?' He made a small sound of regret. 'Obviously your imagination is not as vivid as mine.'

But it was, thought Rachel unhappily. And she could imagine them in bed together only too well. The unbelievable thing was that she should have thought of it, too.

'I don't think we should be having this conversation,' she said at last, taking refuge in her drink. 'What time did you say the electrician would arrive?'

'Not yet.' Gabriel's tone was flat. 'And, for the record, you don't have to worry that I might act on my impulses. However crassly I behaved yesterday, I'm not in the habit of forcing my attentions on anyone.'

Rachel sighed. 'You didn't exactly have to force me,' she admitted honestly. 'But I was angry that you should think I do that all the time. I don't. I—don't know what came over me.'

'I'd like to think it was the same thing that came over me,' remarked Gabriel drily. 'God, Rachel, you know I'm attracted to you. I haven't made any secret of it.'

Rachel took another gulp of her gin and tonic. He'd been right, she thought unsteadily. She did need the lift it gave her. But she still found it hard to accept that Gabriel was sitting here beside her telling her he was attracted to her. Was she being totally naïve? Was he really any different from Joe, no matter what he said?

'I've shocked you,' he said abruptly. 'I seem to have the knack of saying the wrong thing. You'd think I'd learn after the fool I made of myself yesterday. But, dammit, Rachel, can you believe that I was jealous? Jealous of my own son?'

Rachel's throat was dry. 'I told you about Andrew,' she protested. 'I told you I never slept with him.'

'But that doesn't stop me speculating about what did happen between you,' he retorted huskily. 'I know my son—or at least I thought I did. I can't believe he didn't—didn't—'

'Try?' suggested Rachel tightly, and Gabriel gave her a rueful look.

'I guess so,' he said, rolling his glass of beer between his palms. 'Pathetic, isn't it? You'd think at my age I'd know better.'

Rachel bent her head. 'Age has nothing to do with it.'

'No?' Gabriel's tone was ironic. 'I wish I could believe that.' He stared down into his glass, as if hoping to find an answer in its tawny depths. 'I got the feeling yesterday that you never wanted to see me again.'

Rachel shrugged. 'It probably would have been best.'

'Why?' He gazed at her now, his eyes dark with an emotion she didn't dare try to analyse. 'Because I'm too old for you? Because of Andrew? What?'

'Because you are who you are!' she exclaimed, aware that it was important that she didn't hurt him. 'You know what I mean.'

'Do I?' He was being deliberately obtuse, she was sure of it. 'What do you think I want from you, Rachel?'

'I don't know, do I?'

'Sex, is that what you think?' he persisted, and she glanced round a little apprehensively, half afraid that their conversation was audible to other people. But, thankfully, the bar was busy enough for what he'd said to go unnoticed in the general buzz of voices and she relaxed. 'Do you honestly think I'm so desperate to get laid?' he continued, causing the colour to deepen in her cheeks again. 'Dammit, Rachel, I'm not a conceited man, but I'm fairly sure I could find a woman to—to have sex with if I wanted one.' His lips twisted. 'Money can be a great attraction.'

'Not to me.'

'No.' He conceded the fact. 'No, I got that message loud and clear.'

'Good.' Rachel pressed her knees together, uncomfortably aware of the pulse that was beating between her legs. 'I think we'd better go.'

'You haven't finished your drink,' he pointed out flatly. 'And I haven't told you why I wanted to see you.'

Rachel quivered. 'I thought you had.'

'No.' He finished his own beer and slid the empty glass across the bar. 'But perhaps this isn't the right time.' He paused. 'Will you have dinner with me?'

Rachel's lips parted. 'When?'

'Tonight?'

'I can't tonight.'

Her refusal was automatic and, watching his expression, she was fairly sure he knew it. But he didn't question her answer, merely considered a moment before saying, 'Wednesday, then.'

'Wednesday?'

Rachel licked her lips, aware that she had no real reason to refuse him, but Gabriel evidently felt some further explanation was necessary.

'Yes. I can't make it tomorrow,' he replied, and she felt her stomach clench at the expectant look in his eyes.

'I—I'm not sure.'

She was hesitating again and she didn't honestly know why. She couldn't pretend she didn't want to go out with him, because she did. In spite of everything that had happened, in spite of her mother's doubts and Joe Collins' recriminations, she couldn't find it in her heart to reject this man, no matter how crazy that was.

'Rachel...' His use of her name stroked like silk across her sensitive flesh and she trembled. 'Rachel, please...'

'Mr Webb?'

For a moment Rachel was too dazed to identify the source of the strange voice. But then she realised it had come from behind them. A middle-aged man dressed in a short-sleeved tee shirt and corded trousers was standing by Gabriel's stool, and he took a deep breath before turning to give the man an acknowledging nod.

'That's right.'

'I'm George Travis, Mr Webb. I understand you were needing an electrician?'

'Ah, yes.' Gabriel slipped off his stool to confront the man. 'Did Palmer tell you what was needed?'

'He did.' The man nodded. 'But I've left the van parked across the road, so perhaps—Mrs Kershaw—could give me the keys to the café.'

'I'll come with you,' said Rachel at once, sliding her feet to the floor. She looked at Gabriel. 'Um—will you join us?'

'I don't think so.' Gabriel's expression was closed now. 'Good luck with the oven.'

Rachel hesitated, but short of embarrassing all of them she had no choice but to go with George Travis. Apart from anything else, she wanted to hear his opinion of the job Joe had turned down, but she couldn't prevent herself from looking back over her shoulder as she followed the man out of the door.

Gabriel wasn't looking at her, however. Her departure had brought the barman to see if there was anything else he wanted, and Rachel felt an unwilling sense of loss at the sight of Gabriel exchanging a few good-humoured words with the man. What was he saying? she wondered desperately. And when was she likely to see him again?

CHAPTER TEN

THERE were times in the days that followed that Rachel wished she had Gabriel's phone number. Not to encourage him to reissue his invitation to dinner, she assured herself firmly, but simply to thank him for arranging for George Travis to examine the oven. The electrician had told her that there was little wrong with it that he couldn't deal with. One of the elements was worn, he conceded, and would need replacing eventually, but it would last a few months yet. And the switch, which had been causing all the trouble, had been repaired there and then.

Rachel had hardly been able to believe it. The realisation that Joe had been lying to her for reasons of his own was bad enough, but to put her business in jeopardy in the process was unforgivable.

Of course, when she'd told her mother what had happened Mrs Redfern had been predictably suspicious. Her opinion was that as George Travis worked for Gabriel he had probably been told to effect a repair, however temporary it might be. She wouldn't listen when Rachel tried to tell her how unpleasantly Joe had behaved and she persisted in believing that her daughter had exaggerated the whole thing.

Rachel hadn't argued with her for long. There'd been no point, not when her mother refused to even countenance the thought that Gabriel might have had Rachel's best interests at heart. As far as Mrs Redfern was concerned he wasn't to be trusted, and she took every opportunity to persuade Hannah that they were better off not seeing him again.

Then, on Thursday afternoon, just when Rachel had convinced herself that Gabriel had decided he was wasting his time with her, he phoned.

She was in the kitchen of the café at the time, loading dirty plates into the dishwasher, and Patsy came to the open doorway, stretching the cord of the phone behind her.

'It's for you,' she said, and Rachel could tell from her expression that it wasn't her mother. 'It's Mr Webb.'

Rachel nodded, incapable for a moment of making any rational response. Instead, she grabbed a teatowel from the nearby rack and hurriedly wiped her hands.

'I can ask him to ring back,' offered Patsy innocently, but Rachel only gave her a retiring look.

'I'll take it,' she said, putting her hand out for the receiver. Then, with her hand over the mouthpiece, 'Will you finish putting those dishes in the machine?'

Patsy looked put out. 'It's not my job,' she protested.

'Do you want to take it up with your union representative?' asked Rachel shortly, and Patsy pulled a face.

'I don't have a union representative.'

'And you don't have exclusive rights to clearing tables either,' retorted her employer, moving past her. 'Right?'

'All right,' muttered Patsy sulkily, and Rachel heaved a sigh before removing her palm and saying, 'This is Rachel,' into the receiver.

'Hello, Rachel,' said Gabriel mildly. 'Did I ring at a bad time?'

'You might say that,' said Rachel, glancing back at her junior employee. 'But I'm glad you've rung. I've wanted to thank you for what Mr Travis did, and to ask how much I owe you.'

'You don't owe me anything,' Gabriel replied, his tone crisping a little. 'It was done in company time. The company will absorb it.'

'Well—thanks.' Rachel was grateful. She hesitated. 'Was that why you rang?'

'To collect your thanks for the repair of your oven?' Gabriel was sardonic. 'Oh, right. It's been on my mind.'

'Don't be sarcastic!' Rachel spoke unthinkingly, and then

grimaced, thankful that Stephanie had left early; she could imagine what her friend would have made of that. 'I mean— it has been a few days since—since—since it happened.'

'You can't bring yourself to say since I've seen you, can you?' he accused drily. 'But at least you noticed. That's something, I suppose.'

Rachel drew a breath. 'Have—have you been busy?'

'As a matter of fact, I've been away for a couple of days,' he told her flatly. 'I—well, Andrew had got himself into a situation he couldn't deal with, and I—had to bail him out.'

'Oh.' Rachel swallowed. 'Not—literally, I hope?'

'No.' Plainly Gabriel would prefer not to discuss it with her. 'But I'm back now and I wondered if you'd had any second thoughts about having dinner with me.' He paused. 'As I said a few days ago, I would like to talk to you.'

Rachel wanted to say, *About what?* but she knew that would sound crass. And why not admit that she wanted to have dinner with him anyway? At least that way Hannah wouldn't be involved.

'When?' she asked, her palm growing slippery where it gripped the phone. But what would she do if he kissed her again? she was wondering. Could she trust herself not to lose her head as she had before?

'How about tomorrow night?' he suggested, nothing in his tone to indicate that he was especially excited by the prospect. 'I can either pick you up or meet you at Dalziel's. We can have a drink in the bar before the meal.'

Rachel expelled her breath, hardly aware she'd been holding it. Dalziel's was a country club, and its restaurant was probably the most exclusive in the area. Situated on the outskirts of town, it was a select leisure complex that had been built a few years ago. Membership of the sporting facilities which included golf and tennis and squash, was prohibitively expensive, but it was just the sort of place she'd associate with the Webbs.

'You're not changing your mind again?'

His voice had sharpened and Rachel realised she had been silent for far too long. 'Um—Dalziel's,' she murmured doubtfully. 'Isn't that a bit—well, public?'

Now Gabriel was slow to answer her. 'You're ashamed to be seen with me, is that it?' he asked, and she expelled another shaky breath.

'Not at all.'

'It sounds like it to me.'

'Oh, all right.' Rachel gave in. 'What time shall I meet you there? Seven o'clock? Half-past?'

'Make it half-past,' he essayed quietly. 'And don't worry, I'll try not to embarrass you.'

He rang off before she could make any rejoinder and she stared at the dead handset with some frustration before putting it down.

'Can I go now?'

Patsy's defiant enquiry came too close on the heels of Gabriel's cutting their conversation short for her not to have been eavesdropping from the kitchen, and Rachel gave her an impatient look.

'Did you finish filling the dishwasher?'

'And turned it on,' agreed Patsy, taking off her apron. She paused. 'Are you going out with him?'

Rachel was about to say that that was her business, but she didn't want to fall out with the girl. 'As if you didn't know,' she remarked drily, meeting Patsy's indignant gaze with a knowing smile. 'Dalziel's. Have you ever been there?'

'Me?' Patsy squeaked. 'You've got to be joking. Do you know how much it costs to be a member?'

'I can guess.' Rachel was resigned. 'Oh, Lord, what am I going to wear?'

Patsy frowned, evidently taking her question seriously. 'Something sexy,' she said at last. 'The sort of gear that that new shop sells.'

'What new shop?'

'Looking Good,' said Patsy at once, mentioning the name

of a new designer outlet that had opened in the precinct. 'They've got some really gorgeous clothes in there.'

'For women a lot younger than me,' said Rachel flatly, remembering the scantily clad models she'd seen in the window. 'I couldn't wear that sort of thing.'

'Why not?' Patsy regarded her critically. 'If you were fat or overweight I might agree with you. But you could wear anything. Honestly.'

Rachel gave a small smile. 'Flattery will get you everywhere.'

'It's not flattery.' Patsy hesitated. 'I'll come with you, if you like. I know exactly what you need.'

'Well...'

'Of course, if you don't want my help—' began Patsy huffily, and Rachel suppressed a groan. It seemed to be her afternoon for offending people, and she knew Patsy meant well.

'Okay,' she said, once again giving in, in spite of her misgivings. 'If you want to hang on until closing time, I'll be glad of your help.'

But as she drove herself to the country club the following evening Rachel had the uneasy feeling that instead of defying her mother and wearing it, she should have taken her advice and consigned the outfit Patsy had persuaded her to buy to the trash bin. It was much too young for her, and imagining what the other women at the restaurant would be wearing brought her out in a cold sweat.

Yet when she'd looked at her reflection in the mirror back home she'd been pleasantly surprised at how attractive she looked. The thin voile handkerchief top and scallop-hemmed skirt, patterned in shades of blue and green, looked both trendy and elegant. And, teamed with several gold chains and strappy sandals, it gave her a height and sophistication she'd never had before.

It wasn't until she'd gone downstairs and faced her

mother's censure that she'd begun to have doubts, especially when even Hannah had regarded her with worried eyes.

'You look—different, Mummy,' she'd said, and it hadn't been a compliment.

Now, a few hundred metres from her destination, Rachel was convinced she'd made a terrible mistake. But it was too late to turn back now. She would just have to go on and hope Gabriel didn't get the wrong impression. But as she changed gear to turn into the gateway, and noticed how far up her thighs her skirt was riding, she didn't hold out much hope.

She wondered where she was supposed to park her car, but before she could make any decision a uniformed attendant directed her to stop before the impressive entrance and then proceeded to explain that they would park the car for her. Of course, that was after she'd told him she was meeting Mr Gabriel Webb. They didn't just let anyone enter the hallowed portals of Dalziel's, she thought cynically.

Feeling terribly conspicuous, she wrapped the folds of her cashmere scarf more closely about her and mounted the steps to the foyer. Thankfully, it was a warm evening, and she hadn't had to worry about what coat she should wear. And from what she could see of the other guests, her scarf—which, ironically enough, had been a Christmas gift from her mother—was perfectly acceptable. Well, adequate, anyway, she conceded, hoping desperately that Gabriel wasn't going to keep her waiting.

Then she saw him. He was standing at the other side of the foyer, one of a group of more than half a dozen people, all of whom looked perfectly at ease with their surroundings. Most of the women were older than she was, she thought, and their smart suits or silk gowns looked so much more sophisticated than Rachel's simple outfit. She shouldn't have taken Patsy's advice, she fretted. She should have worn something less revealing; something more mature.

Gabriel himself was wearing a pale grey three-piece suit over a dark blue shirt, the colours accentuating the deep tan of his skin. He had never looked more Italian than he did at that moment, she thought, more *alien*, yet at the same time more attractive. Looking at him across the width of the foyer, which was already floodlit despite the earliness of the evening, she knew a sense of disbelief at her own audacity for being there. And, had he not turned his head and seen her, she might well have taken fright and fled.

But he did turn his head, and, meeting his eyes, she was instantly incapable of moving from the spot. Even with more than a dozen people milling between them, she was aware that, however she looked to anyone else, she had found favour in his eyes. The warmth of his approval reached her, surrounded her, left her feeling out of breath and vulnerable.

With an ease she could only admire, he quickly detached himself from the group and strode towards her. He moved with a lithe unconscious grace that attracted more than her attention, and, looking beyond him for a moment, she saw that his departure, and the reason for it, had not gone unnoticed.

'Hi,' he said, reaching her, and Rachel knew a quite outrageous desire to reach up and cover his smiling sensuous mouth with her lips.

That would certainly give his friends something to gossip about, she thought defiantly, but she couldn't do it. 'Hello,' she responded instead. 'Have I kept you waiting long?'

'Dare I say you were worth waiting for?' he asked, taking one of her hands and raising it to his lips. She felt the heated brush of his tongue against her palm and her gaze flew to his, but his eyes were enigmatic. Then, keeping her hand imprisoned in his, he said, 'You look beautiful. I'm very flattered.'

Rachel swallowed. 'Flattered?'

'That you should go to this trouble just for me,' he told her drily. 'Come. I'll introduce you to the president of the club.'

'Oh—no.' Rachel hung back when he would have drawn

her across the lamplit foyer. 'I mean—it's not as if—well, I wouldn't like your friends to get the wrong impression.'

'The wrong impression?' Gabriel's broad shoulders blocked her view of the group of people he had been heading towards. 'How?'

'Oh, you know.' Rachel pulled her hand away and twisted her fingers together. 'What are those people going to think?'

'That I'm a very lucky man?' suggested Gabriel, swaying back on his heels. 'Are you saying you'd rather not be introduced as my—companion?'

'No!' Rachel gazed up at him and then wished she hadn't when she saw the sudden emotion darken his eyes. With a dry mouth she added, 'Oh, Gabriel, I shouldn't be here.'

His mouth twitched. 'Well, at least it got you to use my name,' he remarked softly. 'Come on, Rachel. Tell me how you really feel. Do you wish you hadn't come?'

'I—didn't say that.' Rachel sighed and then, giving in to a totally uncharacteristic burst of vanity, she whispered, 'Do I really look all right? Patsy helped me choose this outfit and—well, I'm sure it's too young for me.'

'It's not.' Gabriel was terse.

'My mother thinks it is.'

'Now, why doesn't that surprise me?' Gabriel blew out a breath. 'You're going out with me, aren't you? That hardly warrants her approval.'

'No, well—' Rachel realised this was the moment she had to confess. 'That's because she thinks you were the reason Andrew and I split up.'

'Me?' He stared at her uncomprehendingly.

'Yes.' Rachel was flushed. 'Oh—if you must know, I was too ashamed to tell her what Andrew had said, so I pretended you had broken us up. Because I wasn't good enough for him.'

Gabriel didn't speak for a few seconds. 'God,' he said at last. 'No wonder she doesn't like me. Don't you think you should tell her the truth?'

'I will. Soon.' Rachel shook her head. 'Do you forgive me? I know it seems pretty pitiful now, but it seemed a good idea at the time.'

'Well, I think we should go and get a drink,' said Gabriel drily. 'And, by the way, you *do* look beautiful. Does that go some way to answering your question?'

Rachel's lips parted, but before she could say anything else Gabriel moved aside and she saw to her relief that the others had disappeared. Probably into the bar, too, she thought uneasily, but she didn't object when Gabriel put his hand in the small of her back and guided her into the reception area.

'The bar's this way,' he directed, and Rachel went with him almost automatically. But she wondered if he was as aware of his fingers against her bare flesh as she was. Unfortunately the cashmere scarf didn't cover much more than her shoulders, and the string ties of her top were no barrier to her smooth skin.

The bar was discreetly lit and intimate, small tables flanked by plush armchairs set on an equally plush carpet. An army of white-coated waiters attended to the needs of its exclusive clientele, and after they were seated Rachel agreed to a glass of white wine before looking nervously about her.

'Relax,' advised Gabriel, loosening the buttons on his jacket and leaning forward, his forearms along his thighs. 'If anyone's under scrutiny here, it's me.'

Rachel permitted herself to look at him. 'Because of me?'

'Indirectly.' Gabriel was ironic. 'They probably think you're the reason I collapsed at my desk.'

Rachel felt her lips tilt upward. 'You don't mean that,' she said, but she could feel herself relaxing anyway. She glanced round again. 'Do you come here a lot?'

'Now there's an original line.' He grinned. 'I wish I'd thought of it.'

Rachel found herself smiling at him. And, because it would be so easy to delude herself into thinking that he really was attracted to her, she hurried into the reason why she was there. 'You—said you wanted to talk to me. About what?'

'I'll get to it,' he said, and then was forced to sit back when the waiter arrived with a Scotch and soda for him and the white wine she had requested for her. He lifted his glass, regarding her over the rim. 'Okay?'

Rachel made a dismissive movement with her shoulders, but she obediently lifted her glass and took a sip of her wine. It was good. Smooth and fruity, with just a taste of dryness, it slid effortlessly down her throat and she thought she could get used to this. After all, he had invited her here, and why shouldn't she enjoy it?

Because it was out of her league, the voice of her conscience reminded her sharply. She shouldn't run away with the idea that she belonged here. Without Gabriel, she wouldn't even have gained entry.

'Mr Webb?'

A waiter was standing diffidently at his elbow and Gabriel looked up in surprise. 'Yes?'

'There's a phone call for you, sir,' the waiter told him. 'Will you take it in the office or shall I bring the phone to your table?'

Gabriel frowned, glancing ruefully at Rachel. 'Do you mind?' He paused. 'If I leave you for a few moments, I mean?'

'I—no.' She did, but she doubted her opinion would make any difference.

'Right.' Gabriel pushed back his chair and got to his feet. 'I won't be long.'

He followed the waiter out of the bar and Rachel was immediately conscious of how isolated she felt. Maybe it would have been better if they'd been sitting with other people, she thought. As it was, she was painfully aware of the fact that she knew no one else here.

'Has he abandoned you?'

The voice startled her. She had been playing with the stem

of her glass, her eyes glued to the table in an attempt to dissociate herself from her surroundings. But now she looked up in surprise to find a slim dark-haired woman standing beside the table. Rachel guessed she was only a few years older than herself, but her poise and elegance gave her a maturity that Rachel could only envy.

'Um—there was a phone call,' she said, and the young woman dropped gracefully into Gabriel's seat.

'You don't mind?' she murmured, but it was a rhetorical question. She held out her hand. 'I'm Louise Paterson. And you are…?'

'Rachel Kershaw,' answered Rachel, shaking Louise's hand. 'How do you do?'

'Oh, I do reasonably well,' replied Louise easily. 'I haven't seen you here before, Miss Kershaw.'

'It's *Mrs* Kershaw,' said Rachel automatically. Then, because she wanted there to be no speculation, 'I'm a widow. But, please, call me Rachel. And, no, I haven't been here before.'

'Well, I must say we're all grateful to you,' remarked Louise surprisingly. 'Gabe's been such an unsociable creature recently. We were beginning to think that nothing would shake him out of his shell.'

Rachel wished she didn't embarrass so easily. 'I'm sure you're exaggerating,' she said, taking a reassuring sip of her wine. 'Um—are you a friend of—of Gabriel's, Miss Paterson?'

'We both are. My husband and myself,' said Louise, subtly asserting her status. 'Are you involved in the pharmaceutical industry, too, Rachel?'

'She doesn't work for me, if that's what you're trying to find out, Louise,' said Gabriel drily, and Rachel looked up at him, the relief evident in her face. She hadn't been aware of his approach and her breath caught in her throat when he casually eased his thigh onto the arm of her chair. 'I gather you've introduced yourselves?'

'Well, as you've been so selfish, keeping her to yourself, I had to do something, darling,' declared Louise, not a bit perturbed at being caught out. Her lids narrowed in knowing speculation. 'Am I intruding?'

'Would I tell you if you were?' Despite the fact that Rachel thought his features were a little more drawn now than they'd been before he'd gone to take the call, Gabriel was perfectly adept at this verbal fencing. 'Where's John? Or shouldn't I ask?'

'Oh, he's networking, as usual,' exclaimed Louise carelessly. She glanced across the room. 'Why don't you and—Rachel—come and join us?'

'Because, as you said, I want to keep her to myself,' replied Gabriel, his hand curving possessively over Rachel's nape. 'Maybe some other time, hmm?'

Rachel's pulse quickened, and it wasn't just because of his hand resting warmly against the back of her neck. Did he mean it? Did he want there to be another time? *Did she?*

'Oh, well...' Louise hid her disappointment behind a mask of mockery. 'I can't remember the last time John said something like that to me.'

'That's probably because you never have time to listen,' remarked Gabriel shrewdly, and she grimaced.

'You men! You always stick together.' And then, realising that someone else had come to join them, 'Oh, there you are, darling. I was just telling Gabriel and his—friend—how you neglect me.'

A much older man stood looking down at them and Rachel realised that this must be Louise's husband. 'Don't you believe it,' he protested heartily. 'She's got me completely under her thumb.'

Gabriel got to his feet to shake the other man's hand. 'Good to see you again, John,' he said politely. 'You're looking well.'

'I wish I could say the same for you,' replied John Paterson rather tactlessly. 'I suppose this is the elusive Mrs

Kershaw? I'd heard that you and she have been seeing one another. How do you do, Mrs Kershaw? I hope my wife hasn't been making a nuisance of herself.'

'No more than usual,' said Louise in a clipped voice, standing up to tuck her hand through her husband's arm. 'Come along, darling. Gabe and Rachel want to be alone.' She arched a mocking brow at Gabriel. 'He said so.'

'Oh, well…'

John Paterson huffed, but although Rachel half expected Gabriel to retract what he'd said, he didn't. Instead he offered them both a smile and then, as they moved away, dropped gratefully down into the seat opposite.

'Sorry about that,' he said, glancing briefly over his shoulder. 'Louise didn't upset you, did she?'

'No.' Rachel was eager to reassure him, as aware of his pallor as John Paterson had been. 'She was very nice, actually.' She paused. 'Is everything all right?'

Gabriel frowned. 'What? Oh—you mean the call. Yes. Yes, everything's fine. Can I order you another drink?'

Rachel refused, sure that everything was not fine, but not confident enough to demand that he share whatever he was concerned about with her. And the arrival of the waiter with their dinner menus halted any further conversation for a while.

'The smoked salmon pâté is good,' Gabriel offered at last, and Rachel gave him a nervous smile.

'Is it? Is that what you're having?'

'No.' Gabriel frowned. 'I think I'll just have salad and a steak.'

'Then I'll have that, too,' declared Rachel, putting the menu aside. 'Um—have you known the Patersons long?'

'Because he's more my age than yours?' Gabriel suggested wryly, and she gave an impatient shake of her head.

'He's much older than you,' she protested. 'Besides, what does that matter?'

'You tell me.'

Gabriel shrugged and emptied his glass just as the waiter returned to take their order. 'You can go through whenever you're ready, Mr Webb,' he said, retrieving the menus. 'I'll send the wine waiter to your table.'

Their table was in the window of the restaurant, overlooking the impressive sweep of the eighteenth tee. It was a beautiful golf course, mused Rachel, the lake she could just see in the fading light and the many trees giving it the ambience of a country park.

'What a lovely view,' she said, hoping to divert Gabriel from whatever was troubling him, and he glanced out of the window briefly before nodding.

'I suppose it is,' he agreed, scanning the wine list. 'Tell me, do you prefer red or white wine?'

'Whatever you like,' said Rachel, sure he must know she was no connoisseur. 'Whenever we have wine, Hannah usually chooses it.'

'Hannah.' Gabriel said her daughter's name slowly, as if she'd reminded him of why they were here, and, after giving the wine waiter his instructions, he leaned back in his seat and regarded her thoughtfully. 'Tell me, how long is it since Hannah had a psychological evaluation?'

Rachel frowned. 'Why do you want to know that?'

Gabriel shrugged. 'Humour me.'

'Well…' Rachel considered. 'I don't remember her ever seeing a psychologist.'

'Never?'

'No.' Rachel was beginning to feel apprehensive. 'She was only three when the accident happened, you know.'

'I know that—' Gabriel broke off for a moment. 'But after what happened on Sunday…'

Rachel pressed her lips together. 'I knew you were going to say that,' she said tensely. 'Is that why you really brought me here? So you could exercise your amateur psychology on me?'

Gabriel scowled. 'You know better than that.'

'Do I?'

'You should.' His mouth tightened. 'And if you'd rather not talk about it, then—'

'Talk about *it*?' Rachel exclaimed. 'Talk about what? The fact that for a few short seconds you got her to stand on her own feet? I don't want to burst your bubble, but I've noticed her moving her legs when she's in the bath. As Dr Williams says, it's only a matter of time before she realises she can walk.'

Gabriel expelled a weary breath. 'If you say so.'

'Well, do you know better?' she demanded. And when he didn't answer her she, too, sighed. 'I'm sorry. I know you mean well, but—oh, I suppose it's a sore topic after—after—'

'After what I said last weekend?' he suggested ruefully. 'Look, it's obvious this is neither the time nor the place to discuss your daughter. I suggest we enjoy our dinner and stop stressing about something that obviously upsets you.'

Rachel wanted to say that it didn't upset her, but she doubted he'd believe her. Yet it was true. She didn't object to him talking about Hannah. She'd got over that. It was just that for years she'd prayed, without any success, that Hannah would regain the use of her legs, and she didn't think she could bear to have her hopes resurrected, only to have them dashed again.

The meal was delicious. The bread was warm and crusty, the salad was crisp, and the steaks were grilled to perfection. Unfortunately, Rachel couldn't do the meal justice, and she found herself drinking more of the wine than she should. But the waiter kept filling her glass and the rich burgundy was giving her a confidence she'd never felt before.

'Tell me something,' Gabriel said, after their plates had been taken away. 'Do you think I brought you here to meet the Patersons?'

Rachel was taken aback. 'Why would I think that?'

'Why not?' Gabriel was watching her closely. 'The older man and his much younger wife.'

'Oh, Gabriel!' This time it was she who reached across the table to capture his hand. 'I don't care about anyone else.'

Gabriel turned his hand so that their fingers were linked together. 'What does that mean? Are you saying you care about me?'

Rachel's tongue clove to the roof of her mouth. 'I—of course I care about you. I care about a lot of people.'

'That wasn't what I meant and you know it.'

She moved her head restlessly from side to side. 'You shouldn't ask me that.'

'Not even if I tell you that I care about you?' His eyes darkened. 'More than I should; I know that.'

Rachel didn't know what to say. 'Is—is that possible?' she asked foolishly, and then realised she was treading deeper and deeper into a veritable minefield of emotion. But she couldn't seem to stop herself.

'That depends on you,' he said now, and then bit off a curse when the waiter reappeared to ask if they would like coffee or pudding. Ignoring the man, he added harshly, 'We could have coffee at my house, if you like.'

'At your house?' Once again Rachel spoke almost involuntarily. 'But I can't. My car—'

'I don't think you should drive home,' declared Gabriel at once, and she wondered briefly if he had had this in mind all along. But when his eyes were pleading with her it was hard to think rationally. 'You're not used to drinking so much wine,' he continued persuasively. 'Please. I'll have my chauffeur collect your car and drive you home again afterwards.'

CHAPTER ELEVEN

AFTER *what*? wondered Rachel apprehensively, as they drove up the drive towards Gabriel's house.

Even the house looked different in moonlight. Although there were lights gleaming from many of the windows, it seemed bigger, darker, and wholly intimidating.

'Your mother?' she ventured before panic overtook her, as the chauffeur swung the Mercedes round in a semi-circle before the door, and Gabriel sighed.

'She's not here,' he said flatly, as if he knew exactly what she was thinking. 'Does it matter?'

'I—assumed she would be,' Rachel murmured, although in all honesty she hadn't thought of the older woman until this moment.

'She's still in London,' Gabriel told her, and as the car stopped he reached for the handle of the door. Then, glancing over his shoulder, he added, 'Are you coming in or do you want me to ask Mario to take you straight home?'

Rachel took a deep breath. On the one hand she was relieved that she wasn't going to have to face the formidable Signora Webb, but, conversely, there was the daunting knowledge that she and Gabriel were alone here. Apart from his staff, of course, though she doubted they'd have much sympathy with her predicament.

Her predicament?

Rachel gave an impatient shake of her head. She was taking this far too seriously. She wasn't a child, for heaven's sake, and she was perfectly capable of taking care of herself.

'I—thought you were going to offer me coffee,' she said firmly, shifting forward on the seat. 'Besides, Mario is going to collect my car, isn't he?' She paused. 'If he doesn't mind.'

Gabriel gave a small smile. 'Oh, I think I can assure you that Mario will be happy to collect your car and take you home whenever you wish,' he remarked drily, exchanging a knowing look with the chauffeur. 'Shall we go?'

An older woman Rachel hadn't seen on her first visit met them in the reception hall. Tonight the chandelier was in darkness and the only illumination came from concealed lighting high up on the walls. But it was enough to see that the woman was surprised to see them, though her real feelings were carefully concealed.

'Mr Webb,' she said politely. 'We didn't expect you back so soon.' Her eyes moved curiously to his companion. 'Is there anything I can get for you, sir?'

'Yes. Coffee for two,' said Gabriel easily. Then, to Rachel, 'This is Mrs Hamilton, my housekeeper. You'll find she's a real treasure.'

The woman smiled, but Rachel doubted she'd ever have the opportunity to decide one way or the other. 'How do you do?' she said, not sure what the protocol was in circumstances like this. 'It's very nice to meet you.'

'And you, Miss—Mrs—?'

'Kershaw,' supplied Gabriel swiftly. 'Mrs Kershaw.' He glanced round. 'We'll have coffee on the patio, Mrs Hamilton. As soon as you can, right?'

'Yes, sir.'

The housekeeper sounded willing enough, but Rachel felt her eyes upon them as Gabriel ushered her across the hall and into a large sitting room she hadn't seen before. He switched on a couple of lamps before closing the double-panelled doors behind them, and Rachel breathed a little more easily now that they were alone.

Which was probably very stupid!

'Oughtn't you to have told her I'm a widow?' she asked now, glancing over her shoulder, and Gabriel pulled a wry face.

'I don't have to explain myself to my staff,' he replied,

moving to the windows and opening the long glass doors that gave onto the patio. He pushed them wide. 'Are you coming?' he asked, pressing another switch to flood the area beyond with a mellow golden light.

Holding her scarf about her, Rachel stepped outside and was immediately assailed by the scent of a dozen night-flowering blossoms. Pots of geraniums, hanging baskets of fuchsia and lobelia, trellises hung with vines, gave the whole scene a distinctly foreign appearance, and she guessed his mother must have had a hand in its creation.

Beyond the patio, the swimming pool they had seen the previous week as they'd walked to the stables glinted invitingly, and once again she was reminded of Hannah. After all, the only reason she had come here on that occasion had been to please her daughter. She should remember that and not fool herself by imagining that this was anything more than a fleeting diversion.

'It's a beautiful night,' remarked Gabriel softly, and she glanced his way. He had shed his jacket onto one of the rattan chairs that were set in the shade of a rose-covered pergola and unfastened the top button of his shirt. He was presently tugging his tie a couple of inches away from his collar when he caught her looking at him. 'Is something wrong?'

Nothing. *Everything*, thought Rachel breathlessly, aware of how attractive he looked now that he had shed the formality he had worn in the restaurant. 'What could be wrong?' she offered, wishing she had more experience in these situations. 'It's very warm, isn't it?'

'You'd noticed.' His tone was mocking. 'You wouldn't think so to judge by the way you're clinging to your scarf.'

'Oh.' Rachel's arms slackened and the scarf fell about her waist. 'I wasn't thinking.'

'I think you were thinking too much,' retorted Gabriel drily, and she started when he pressed another switch so that the pool was suddenly lit from below the water. 'Relax.'

The return of Mrs Hamilton with the coffee Gabriel had

ordered gave her a few moments to escape the knowledge
that she couldn't hide from him. But she had to keep her
head, she told herself fiercely, even if it would be incredibly
easy to allow the beauty and the sensuality of her surroundings to seduce her reason. 'Is there anything else I can get
for you, sir?' Mrs Hamilton asked, stepping back from the
table where she had set the tray and regarding him expec-
tantly. 'Er—will Mrs Kershaw be staying the night?'

'No!' Rachel's shocked denial prevented Gabriel from
making some ambiguous statement that might give the
woman the wrong impression. 'No, I'll be leaving after we've
had coffee.'

'Yes, madam.' Mrs Hamilton inclined her head. 'I'll see
you in the morning, then, Mr Webb. Goodnight. Goodnight,
Mrs Kershaw.'

'Goodnight.'

Only Gabriel's response was audible and Rachel wondered
if he was annoyed at her hasty reply. But it wasn't evident
in his voice when he asked if she would like cream or sugar,
and she glanced round to find him pouring some of the fil-
tered coffee into bone china cups.

'Um—black, please,' she said, keeping the width of the
table between them, and Gabriel gave her a weary look.

'In case the wine might have gone to your head, is that
right?' he suggested drily. 'Don't worry. I can keep my baser
impulses in check.'

'I—I—you're embarrassing me,' she said awkwardly, and
he gave her a cynical look.

'You don't think that jumping in to assure Mrs Hamilton
that you'll be leaving just as soon as you can swallow this
coffee is embarrassing to me?'

Rachel coloured. 'I—perhaps,' she conceded, dropping her
scarf on the chair behind her. 'I'm sorry. I shouldn't have
come.'

'And that's what this is really all about, isn't it?' he demanded flatly. 'You're afraid because we're alone here. Afraid of what I might do to you.'

'I'm not afraid.' She was indignant.

'No?' He obviously didn't believe her. 'Well, if you're not afraid of me, who are you afraid of? Yourself?'

Rachel lifted her shoulders. 'I—maybe,' she conceded, almost without thinking, and he groaned.

'Rachel…'

He moved round the table towards her, but when he would have reached for her she almost jack-knifed away from him. She knew if he touched her she'd be lost, but Gabriel didn't see it that way.

He swore then, audibly this time, before raking long fingers over his scalp. 'Drink your coffee,' he advised harshly, starting across the patio. He flung off his waistcoat and it dropped to the floor at her feet. 'I won't be long.'

'But where are you going?'

Rachel was anxious now, and the look he cast back over his shoulder was full of bitterness. 'Does it matter?' he asked, his fingers unbuttoning his shirt. Then, as she continued to stare after him, 'I'm going for a swim. I need to cool off.'

'A swim?' Rachel was shocked. 'But—is that wise?'

'Wise?' Gabriel's voice floated back to her as he descended the steps to the apron that surrounded the pool. 'Oh, right. Because my mother's convinced you I've been ill?' he called mockingly. 'Well, why should that concern you? It isn't as if you care.'

But she did!

Rachel fretted at the thought, but it was true. As he stripped off his shirt and stepped out of his trousers her heart ached with the knowledge of how much. But it was foolish, she told herself, watching him kick off his shoes and socks. She and Gabriel were never going to be more than friends.

He paused and looked back at her then, and she quickly looked away. She was feeling very much like a voyeur, but the image of his lean muscled body wouldn't be dislodged.

Common sense was telling her she should demand that he send for Mario and allow her to go home. It surely couldn't take long for him to drive to and from the country club. But the knowledge of how she had felt in the restaurant—how she still felt now, if she was honest with herself—kept her silent.

'Would you like to join me?' he called, but she shook her head.

'No, thanks.'

He said nothing more, but the sound of his body cleaving the water brought her head round. She'd been half afraid he was naked, but as she watched him swim strongly underwater towards the far end of the pool she could see he was still wearing his shorts. Green silk boxers clung to the tight curve of his buttocks, clearly visible in the concealed light.

Rachel felt a frightening surge inside her, a realisation that this man had come to mean more to her than she'd ever dreamed it was possible to feel. Dear God, she acknowledged with a sense of panic, she was falling in love with him. Now, how stupid was that?

Gabriel had swum to the end of the pool and was now swimming back, his dark head barely clearing the water. He wasn't looking at her, he was concentrating on his stroke, and, almost unaware of what she was doing, Rachel moved to the top of the steps that led down to the pool.

She waited until he reached the apron and then, her arms wrapped closely about her waist, she said stiffly, 'Do you think Mario will be back yet?'

Gabriel's mouth compressed. 'Have you drunk your coffee?'

'I don't want it,' she answered tightly. 'I don't like drinking alone.'

'Don't you?' With a lithe movement Gabriel vaulted out of the pool to stand dripping water onto the tiled surround. 'I got the impression you didn't want my company either.'

Rachel quivered. 'I didn't say that.'

'No.' His tone was wry as he climbed the steps towards her and she stiffened. She was sure he intended to touch her, and this time she had no idea how she would respond. But he merely brushed past her, his damp skin chill against her arm, saying over his shoulder, 'I'll get dressed.'

He disappeared into the house and Rachel allowed the breath she had been holding to disperse. And, as she did so, she realised he'd left his clothes strewn in a path towards the pool. With an exclamation of concern she hurriedly gathered them all together, and then, although she wasn't at all sure what she intended to do with them, she went after him.

He wasn't in the sitting room, or in the spacious entrance hall that had so impressed her the week before. Nor was there any sign of Mrs Hamilton, though Rachel thought that that at least wasn't a disadvantage. She had no real desire to meet Gabriel's housekeeper with her arms full of Gabriel's clothes, however innocent it might be.

The staircase rose imposingly on her right and she paused at its foot to stare doubtfully up into its shadowy heights. Lamps were lit along its length, but they barely illuminated more than each individual step. Yet she was sure that Gabriel had gone up them. A trace of moisture clinging to the banister told of his passage, and, without giving herself time to think, Rachel started up the stairs.

A galleried landing confronted her at the top of the stairs, circling three sides of the hall below before heading off in several directions. A soft carpet cushioned her feet, silenced her footsteps, and she turned uncertainly from side to side, not sure where Gabriel had gone.

The sound of running water drew her along the corridor to her right, an open door into what appeared to be a suite of rooms giving her an unmistakable clue. Gabriel was obviously taking a shower after his swim in the pool, and she quickly laid his clothes on the huge square bed and prepared to leave.

'Rachel!'

The water was still running and she turned a startled face towards the bathroom door. Gabriel stood there, a towel wrapped hastily about his hips, his expression a mingling of disbelief and expectation.

'I—you left your clothes—outside,' she said, her face flaming with embarrassed colour. 'I—I didn't intend to intrude—'

'You're not.' One hand moved from his flat midriff to his shoulder and back again, almost nervously. He glanced behind him. 'I was going to have a shower.'

'Yes.'

Rachel was intensely aware of the movement of his hand, of the way his long fingers disturbed the light covering of hair on his chest. Hair that arrowed down to his navel and beyond. When he'd kissed her in the stables those same fingers had touched her, caressed her. The lean strength of his thighs had pressed against hers and she'd felt the powerful thrust of his arousal against her stomach. She suspected he was aroused now, and she couldn't prevent her eyes from seeking the proof concealed by the loosely knotted towel.

God, why was she thinking of that now?

'I—I'll wait for you downstairs,' she began, but she knew as Gabriel came towards her that this time she had gone too far. The confirmation was in his eyes, and when he reached for her she had no defence to offer.

'Stay,' he said huskily, cupping her face in his hands, and when his mouth found hers she could only give in to her own urgent need to be close to him.

Her hands uncurled against the damp skin of his waist, her breasts crushed against the muscled strength of his chest. She had never been this close to any man except Larry, and she couldn't remember him inspiring the feelings inside her that Gabriel so effortlessly aroused. Everywhere he touched, a spark of electricity seemed to jump from his flesh to hers, and, although she had never considered herself a sensual woman, she found herself arching against him, wanting to feel every inch of his taut frame moulded to hers.

'God, Rachel,' he said hoarsely, gathering her closer. 'Do you have any idea how much I want you?'

Rachel took a trembling breath. 'I think so,' she whispered, her fingers gripping his neck. Then, as he pulled the ties that held her top in place, 'Ought—oughtn't we to close the door?'

'No one's going to disturb us,' he assured her as his hands found her breasts. 'God, you're beautiful,' he added as his palms caressed her swollen nipples. 'So beautiful!'

Rachel felt dizzy with emotion. So dizzy, in fact, that when he drew her across to the huge bed she was almost relieved to subside onto the cool coverlet. She thought perhaps the coverlet was made of satin, it was so smooth and sensuous against her hot skin. But she paid it little heed when Gabriel came down beside her and kissed her neck.

Then his mouth was on hers again, his tongue pressing urgently between her teeth to take possession of the moist cavern within. His kiss was deep, passionate, seducing her as surely as the hands that had taken possession of her body.

She wasn't wearing a bra, and her skirt was soon disposed of. But, although she'd expected him to go ahead and strip off her panties, too, he didn't. Instead he parted her legs, and kneeling between them, he bent and suckled at each of her breasts in turn.

Fire shot through her at the sensual tugging of his tongue and his teeth. Her nipples felt hot and tender, her breasts heavy with longing. She found herself surging up on her elbows to make it easier for him, lifting her breasts to his mouth, moaning with satisfaction at the pleasure he was giving her.

When his mouth moved from her breasts to follow a sensuous path to her navel she almost groaned with disappointment. She wanted him to go on with what he'd been doing, but then his tongue probed the hollow above her abdomen and she was instantly receptive to other sensations. Wherever he touched she was made aware of receptors she'd hardly known she possessed, and now she ached for him to move even lower.

And he did. With unhurried skill, he bent to peel her panties away from the triangle of hair that hid her womanhood. But only so far. Although she was fretting for him to go further, he seemed content to stroke the increasingly damp curls, and only when she uttered an agonised cry did he slide his fingers down into her sweetness.

'Please,' she said then, gazing up at him, and he arched his brow in that familiar frustrating way he had when he teased her.

'What?' he asked softly, but she knew he knew exactly what she wanted. 'Do you want me to take these off?' he continued, flicking the elastic trim. And when she nodded he smiled. 'You do it,' he said. 'You do it for me.' And with trembling fingers she struggled up and did so.

'Ah, Rachel,' he groaned then, and she realised that that simple action had achieved what all her silent pleading had not. 'Tell me you want me.'

'I want you. I want you,' she said, in a desperate breathless voice.

He entered her then, smoothly and slickly, her own quivering flesh making it easy for him. She'd been half afraid he would hurt her, but he didn't. She was more than ready for him, and his pulsating length fitted perfectly into her wet sheath. She would have liked for him to stay there for a while, allowing her to enjoy the sensation of him filling her so completely, but Gabriel was past the point of no return. His carnal energies were driving him on, and with a muffled groan he started to move.

'I'm sorry,' he said against her neck as he pulled almost fully out of her before plunging in again and alerting all the little sexual sensors inside her. His teeth tugged on her soft flesh. 'I've wanted you for so long...'

'Me, too,' she confessed helplessly, turning her lips against his roughening jawline, and he uttered a moan of triumph as the first shudders of her release triggered his.

Some time later, Rachel stirred to the awareness that it must be very late. She suspected she must have fallen asleep after their lovemaking, and although she was loath to move and disturb Gabriel, who was slumbering so contentedly beside her, she knew she had to go home.

She groaned as she thought of Gabriel's chauffeur, who must have been waiting for hours, and despite the wantonness of her behaviour she felt the deepening heat stain her neck at the knowledge that he must know exactly what had been going on.

Was he used to it? she wondered uneasily. Was she just one of many women that Gabriel had brought here? Although she didn't want to face it, he had never denied that there had been other women in his life.

The thought spurred her into action and, although one of Gabriel's legs was imprisoning her to the bed, she attempted to slide away. But his face was pillowed on the tangled mass of her hair, and when she moved he opened his eyes.

'Where are you going?' he protested, his hand closing possessively around her arm, and when she parted her legs to give her leverage, his thigh slid intimately between.

'I have to go home,' she murmured, instantly aware of his muscled power brushing the sensitive nub of her femininity and desperately wanting to respond to it. 'Don't you get up. I can find my own way home.'

'Yeah, right.' He was sardonic, rolling over to cover her quivering body with his. His hand cupped her nape. 'Do you honestly think I'd let you go alone?'

'I—' Rachel was overpoweringly aware of his stirring arousal. 'Gabriel, I don't want to go, but—'

'Then don't,' he said simply, lowering his mouth to nuzzle her throat. 'I'll take you back myself in the morning.'

'I—can't let you do that—'

'No, she can't,' a strange voice inserted harshly. 'God, Dad, I wondered why Nonna advised me to stay away from Copleys. I thought it was because of what I'd done. I didn't realise you wanted to leave the way clear so that you could screw my ex-girlfriend. I know you told Nonna you felt sorry for her, having a disabled kid and all, but isn't this carrying sympathy a tad too far?'

CHAPTER TWELVE

'I TOLD you no good would come of it.'

With her mother's words ringing in her ears, Rachel made a concerted effort to concentrate on shaping the ready-made mixture into scones. It was a job she normally enjoyed: taking the pre-prepared dough out of the freezer and making it into the mouth-watering cakes that had been her first success when she'd opened the café. But this morning she was impatient and on edge, and she would have given a great deal not to have had to open up today.

But that would have been stupid, and she knew it. Whatever kind of mess she was making of her private life, the café was her livelihood, hers and Hannah's, and she wasn't going to do either of them any favours by allowing what had happened on Friday night to ruin her business.

All the same, it was incredibly difficult to keep her mind on her job. It was just as well that she'd left home earlier than usual, because she was probably going to have to scrap this first batch of scones and start over. Her reputation depended on not letting her customers down, and she owed it to Stephanie and Patsy, too, not to jeopardise their jobs.

Even so, she dreaded the moment when Stephanie would turn up for work. Her friend knew her so well, and, despite frequent visits to the bathroom to douse her eyes with cold water, Rachel suspected the other woman would know immediately that she'd been crying. Which in itself was stupid, too, but she couldn't help it.

She supposed it was a case of delayed reaction. Somehow she'd managed to keep herself together over the weekend, even when Gabriel had done the unthinkable and turned up at the house. Of course he'd wanted to know why she wasn't at the café, but she hadn't answered the door. With a cowardice that was new to her she had begged her mother to speak to him in her stead, to tell him what Rachel had told Stephanie earlier: that she was unwell and unable to work today.

She'd half expected him to insist on seeing her, and in those circumstances there was no telling what her mother might have done. After all, for all her belligerence, Mrs Redfern was not unaware of Gabriel's influence in the town, and Rachel was sure he could be intimidating if he chose to be so.

But in the event he'd accepted her mother's excuses and gone away, leaving Mrs Redfern with the perfect excuse for her I-told-you-so attitude.

Which, in its way, had helped Rachel to maintain her own composure. So long as her mother expected her to fall apart, she felt obliged to prove her wrong, but now, away from her, and Hannah's childishly knowing eyes, she'd gone to pieces, and she didn't know how she was going to pull herself together again.

She felt the tears pricking at her eyes again and she struggled to blink them back. Her customers wouldn't appreciate having their morning scones laced with salt, she thought, trying to find some humour in the situation. But there was none. She was totally without humour; totally without hope.

She sniffed, turning away to snatch a paper towel from the roll and rub frantically at her eyes. God, she was going to look such a sight! People were bound to think there'd been a death in the family. And what did it say about her that she almost felt as if there had?

The bell pealed and she glanced towards the door, panic in her eyes. It was too early for Stephanie, definitely too early for Patsy. So...

It was him. As she'd half known it would be. And she wanted to die of embarrassment. She should have locked the door behind her, she thought uselessly. She should have taken the fact that she was much earlier than usual into account, instead of assuming, as she usually did, that Stephanie wouldn't be far behind her.

Gabriel didn't make that mistake. With evident forethought he dropped the latch behind him, successfully forestalling any interruption. Or any chance of evasion, she acknowledged bitterly, half ashamed now that she had allowed her mother to get rid of him on Saturday morning. She should have faced him then, instead of chickening out of something that exposed her weakness, not his.

Determinedly blowing her nose on the paper towel she had used to wipe her eyes, Rachel thrust it into the wastebin before turning to face him. Let him think what he liked, she thought painfully. He and his son had probably already had a laugh at her expense. She thanked God that Mario had collected her car and left it parked on the forecourt in front of Gabriel's house with the keys still in the ignition.

'Are you prepared to listen to me now?'

Although she'd expected him to say something like that, Rachel was surprised by the roughness of his tone. If she hadn't known better she'd have wondered if he wasn't struggling with some uncontrollable emotion of his own, though she guessed this must be a new experience for him: trying to justify actions that were totally unjustifiable.

'I suppose so. If I must,' she replied, her eyes shifting away from his penetrating gaze. 'But I hope you understand that, whatever you say, I can't promise to believe you.'

'Fair enough.' Gabriel's tone was flat now. 'But at least give me the benefit of a hearing, without running away.' His lips curled with sudden irony. 'I was half afraid you'd have brought your mother with you to run interference.'

Rachel held up her head. 'My mother was only doing what I asked her to do.'

'And saying what you asked her to say?' Gabriel rested both hands on the counter between them. 'Yeah, I gathered that.'

'So?' Rachel forced herself to look at him again, hoping she didn't look half as haggard as she felt. 'You must have realised that, whatever you and Andrew have come up with, I'm not likely to believe it.'

'Rachel!' Gabriel's jaw clenched and his hands curled into fists on the Formica surface. 'I can see you're upset, so don't pretend that what happened between us didn't mean anything to you. It did. It meant something to me, too. And I certainly haven't discussed our relationship with my son.'

'No?' Somehow she managed to inject a sceptical note into her voice. 'But you must have discussed me with your mother. What was it Andrew said? That she'd told him you felt sorry for me? Yes, that was it. Well, here's a newsflash: I don't need your pity!'

Gabriel sighed. 'Would you believe me if I told you I'd said nothing to my mother? Anything she's relayed to Andrew is her interpretation of the situation, not mine.'

Rachel's lips twisted. 'Oh, right.'

'It's true.' His voice harshened. 'For God's sake, Rachel, you've got to believe me. I didn't come here today to let you stonewall me again. Okay, what happened was—unfortunate, unpleasant, even, but I had no idea Andrew would turn up as he did.'

'No, I believe that.' Rachel was bitter. 'I'm sure the last thing you wanted was for your son to see you in such a—a compromising situation.'

'It wasn't compromising,' exclaimed Gabriel angrily. 'Not to me, anyway.' He paused, and when she didn't say anything he went on doggedly, 'As I say, when I'd spoken to Andrew earlier in the evening he was still in London, and I'd assumed—mistakenly as it turned out—that he intended to stay there. But, as always, Andrew doesn't care about anyone's feelings but his own, and he'd decided that stating his case in person might—might change my mind.'

'Change your mind?' Rachel knew she shouldn't ask the

question, knew she should show no interest in his affairs, but she couldn't help herself.

'Yes.' Gabriel flexed his shoulders. 'He—well, he wants me to—to increase his allowance.'

'And he drove down from London in the middle of the night to tell you that?' Rachel stared at him disbelievingly. 'Oh, right. I believe that.'

'Andrew's problems are nothing to do with us.'

'No, they're not.' Rachel's voice was tremulous. 'Nothing to do with you and your family is anything to do with me. Thank you for reminding me.'

'That wasn't what I meant.' Gabriel groaned. 'What I meant was—'

'Don't bother to go on,' said Rachel unsteadily. 'I don't want to hear whatever lies you've concocted to explain why your son would turn up in the middle of the night and find us in bed together. Perhaps Andrew had it right. Perhaps you did want to keep him away until you'd got me into bed. It might even have been some kind of game you were playing between you. He didn't succeed, but you did.'

'It wasn't anything like that and you know it,' snapped Gabriel savagely. 'All right. I'll tell you why Andrew really wanted to see me—'

Rachel whirled away, putting her hands over her ears. 'I don't want to hear—'

'No, but you're going to,' he snarled, coming round the counter and catching her as she would have disappeared into the kitchen. Dragging her arms away from her ears, he twisted them behind her, backing her up against the wall beside the ovens. 'You're going to listen to me if I have to gag you to do so.'

Rachel was trembling. 'Let me go.'

'Not yet.'

'Stephanie will be here soon.'

'So she'll hear it, too. It's about time she realised you're not the only victim in this relationship.'

Rachel tried to twist away. 'You're not a victim.'

'Aren't I?'

'No.' She lifted her head and somehow managed to stare at him. 'You know what you are? You're no better than Joe Collins!'

It was an unforgivable thing to say, an unforgivable accusation to make. As soon as the words were out of her mouth Rachel regretted them. Whatever his faults, Gabriel was not like Joe Collins. He had never been dishonest with her or cheated her, and if she no longer trusted him that was more her fault than his.

But it was too late. Whatever he had been about to say, whatever excuses he had been about to make, Gabriel had evidently had enough. With a violent oath he thrust himself away from her, his hands dropping woodenly to his sides.

'Perhaps you're right,' he said, and for a moment she thought he was admitting that he was no better than Joe. But then he continued contemptuously, 'Perhaps my problems are nothing to do with you. I've been wasting my time thinking that you might be suffering because of what I did, when in fact you're more concerned with what Andrew might have thought of your behaviour.'

'That's not true!' Rachel was appalled that he should have got her so completely wrong. 'I don't care about Andrew—'

'The trouble is, I don't think you care about anybody,' retorted Gabriel sadly, striding towards the door. He lifted the latch. 'G'bye, Rachel. Oh, and give Hannah my love.'

How Rachel got through the next couple of weeks, she never knew. She supposed that habit made a good ally, and, despite the fact that she was torn apart inside, outside organisation and routine enabled her to function with a fair degree of success.

Her mother knew that all was not well, of course, and despite her earlier threats to wash her hands of the whole affair she'd proved a good friend again. Indeed, Rachel didn't know how she'd have managed without her.

It had helped that she'd confided the real reason she and Andrew had split up to her mother. That it had been his unwillingness to accept Hannah as part of Rachel's life that had caused the rift between them and not anything his father had said. Andrew's opinion had been that if Rachel hoped to continue with their relationship she should seriously consider putting Hannah into a home, and Rachel had had no hesitation in telling him what she thought of that. Besides, she had already been having doubts about other aspects of his character, and if the break-up had been no less painful, it was her pride that had suffered the most.

Then, towards the end of the second week after that awful scene with Gabriel, something happened to bring her out of the trough of despair into which she'd sunk.

She got a call from Hannah's school. The head teacher, Mrs Gower, rang the café on Friday lunchtime to ask Rachel if she could come and pick up her daughter herself that day. She wouldn't say much more over the phone, except to assure Rachel that Hannah was perfectly all right, but for the rest of the afternoon, until it was time for her to go to the school, Rachel was in a state of nerves.

'You have no idea what she wants?' Stephanie asked curiously, once Rachel had come off the phone after ringing her mother to tell her of the new arrangements. 'You didn't even tell your mother that Hannah's head teacher had asked you to go.'

'I know.' Rachel knew a momentary sense of guilt. 'But I didn't think there was any point in worrying her when it might be nothing important.'

'Yet you don't believe that,' observed Stephanie shrewdly. 'I know you, Rachel. You're already anticipating the worst.'

'Well, wouldn't you be?' Rachel was indignant.

'After what happened between you and Gabriel Webb?' Stephanie only knew that she and Gabriel had had a row and split up. The fact that Andrew Webb was back at Copleys hadn't been mentioned, but Rachel guessed that Stephanie thought he had had something to with it. And he had. Only not directly. 'Well, okay, I suppose it has been a pretty rough couple of weeks.'

Rachel turned away. 'I'll survive,' she said tightly. 'You don't mind staying on this afternoon, do you?'

Stephanie pulled a face. 'What was it you just said? I'll survive?' she remarked drily. 'Now, stop worrying about something that may never happen. Hannah's probably had a fall or cut herself in needlework. You know how fussy head teachers can be.'

'Do you think so?'

Rachel tried to console herself with her friend's words, but it was little comfort in the taxi she took out to St Winifred's later that afternoon. Hannah had fallen before, and cut herself, too, on occasion. But Mrs Gower had never asked her to come to the school before.

'Please, wait,' she told the taxi driver when they reached the school. 'I shouldn't be more than ten or fifteen minutes.'

Or she hoped not, she thought tensely as she went through the automatic doors that led into the school's entrance hall. Like everything else at St Winifred's, the doors were geared to make things easy for their wheelchair-bound pupils, and it was one of the first things that had persuaded Rachel to choose this school for her daughter.

Mrs Gower's secretary showed her into the head teacher's office. It was still fifteen minutes to the end of the school day and Rachel hoped to get this—whatever it was—over with before going to collect Hannah.

They shook hands and then the older woman indicated the chair at the opposite side of her desk. 'Please, sit down, Mrs Kershaw,' she said easily. 'Can I offer you a cup of tea?'

'Nothing, thanks.' Rachel was too on edge to want any refreshment. 'Um—I have a taxi waiting. Could we possibly get to the reason why you asked me to come here?'

'Of course, of course.' Mrs Gower seemed to understand her apprehension. 'I'll get straight to the point: how long has Hannah been able to move around?'

Rachel's jaw dropped. 'Move around?' she echoed blankly. 'You mean, how long has she been able to handle her wheelchair? Oh, a few years. As you know—'

'Not her wheelchair,' interrupted Mrs Gower steadily. 'I meant, how long has she been able to get out of her chair without any assistance?'

'She doesn't. She can't.' Rachel stared at the woman with wide disbelieving eyes. And then, reading Mrs Gower's expression, 'You mean, she has?'

'So I'm told,' agreed the head teacher, nodding. She rested her forearms on her desk and linked her fingers together. 'I gather you know nothing about it?'

'No.' But Rachel was instantly reminded of that day at Copleys, and of how proud Hannah had been of her achievement. 'That is, she did stand once. But that was with—someone's assistance.'

Mrs Gower considered her words. 'And do you think this might have encouraged her to try it again? On her own?'

'I—don't know.' Rachel was stunned and trying not to show it. 'How—how did you find out?'

'Ah.' Mrs Gower released her hands and lay back in her chair. 'Unfortunately it seems she has grown a little too confident of her own abilities. During her painting lesson this morning she apparently dropped her paintbrush, and because Mrs Wilson was otherwise engaged Hannah attempted to pick it up herself.'

Rachel's jaw dropped. 'She fell?'

'Only a little way.' Mrs Gower seemed unperturbed by that aspect of the incident. 'But it did acquaint us with the evident improvement in her condition. And, according to her classmates, Hannah has got out of her chair on more than one occasion. You say you've had no inkling that her paralysis may be responding to therapy?'

'I—no.'

But then for the past couple of weeks Rachel had been so wrapped up in her own misery that she'd paid only nominal attention to her daughter.

'Well, I do believe Hannah wanted to surprise you. That's what she says, anyway.' Mrs Gower paused. 'I had her checked over by our own doctor after the fall and he assures me that no harm has been done. In fact...' She hesitated. 'That was why I asked you to come in. It seems obvious from recent events that Hannah's condition may be self-induced, and Dr Rigsby wants me to suggest that you allow her to talk to a counsellor.'

'A counsellor?'

'A child psychologist,' clarified Mrs Gower quickly. 'It's possible that the child is suppressing something—some incident that happened either at the time of the accident or just before it—which may have caused her to become paralysed in the first place.'

It was ironic, Rachel thought, as they were driven home later that afternoon, that the school doctor should say much the same thing as Gabriel and Gabriel's mother. Were it not such a ludicrous proposition she might have wondered if Gabriel had had any part in that conclusion, but, however far-reaching the Webbs' influence might be, she doubted if he had any further interest in Hannah's treatment. Since that morning at the café she had neither heard nor read anything about him or Andrew, and she'd told herself with increasing desperation that nor did she want to.

But Hannah was another matter, and, although she said little to the child in the taxi, as soon as they got home, and Mrs Redfern had been assured that her granddaughter was well, Rachel demanded that Hannah tell her what had been going on.

'You know,' said the little girl sulkily, apparently in no mood to demonstrate her motor skills to her mother and grandmother. 'Mrs Gower told you.'

'Told you what?' asked Rachel's mother, and Rachel swiftly explained why the head teacher had wanted to see her.

'You can stand?' exclaimed Mrs Redfern, staring at the child as if she couldn't believe her eyes. 'Why didn't you tell us?'

''Cos you didn't want to know,' said Hannah indifferently. 'I told you I could stand that day Mummy and me went to Gabe's house, but Mummy told me not to do it again.'

'I didn't—'

'Yes, you did.' Hannah was indignant. 'It was when Katy took me to see the horses. You said I couldn't show her what I'd done.'

Rachel groaned. 'That was different.'

'No, it wasn't.' Hannah stared at her. 'And Katy said that if I couldn't walk, I couldn't ride one of the horses either, so—so—'

'So you decided you would,' Rachel finished for her weakly. 'Oh, baby, why didn't you tell me?'

'I'm not a baby,' retorted Hannah with a sniff. 'And I am going to walk again. One day. I know you said we couldn't go to Copleys again, but maybe if I could walk Gabe would change his mind.'

'Oh, Hannah!' Rachel exchanged a helpless look with her mother over the child's head. Then, stifling the sudden urge to burst into tears herself, she added, 'Just—just wait until I tell Mrs Stone what a clever girl you are.'

CHAPTER THIRTEEN

RACHEL worried about what Hannah had said all weekend. It was impossible to dissociate her daughter's words from the opinion of the doctor at St Winifred's, and Rachel was in the unhappy position of knowing that she had brought everything that had happened on herself. Of course she wanted Hannah to recover the use of her legs, to walk again, to be doing all the things a little girl of her age should be doing, but not like this. Maybe she was selfish, but she couldn't help wishing that Gabriel Webb hadn't been involved.

Walking to the bus stop on Monday morning, Rachel had still not reconciled herself to the knowledge that, without Gabriel's intervention, it could have been months or even years before Hannah attempted to use muscles that had been weakened by her paralysis. God knew, she might never have had the courage to do what she'd done. Until Gabriel had gained her confidence, until he had offered her the prospect of a totally new experience, she had seemed quite content with her lot.

Or perhaps that was simplifying matters too much. The truth was Hannah probably couldn't remember a different way of life, and Rachel had to admit she had accepted the physiotherapist's gloomy diagnosis that her daughter was lazy. In the beginning Dr Williams had been optimistic, but even he had stopped making any unrealistic promises, and, in spite of what she'd told Gabriel, Rachel had begun to doubt that Hannah would ever walk again.

Now there was a genuine possibility. Rachel had phoned Dr Williams on Saturday morning and he was going to make an appointment for Hannah to see a child psychologist. He'd accepted the other doctor's opinion with genuine interest, and, although she doubted he thought it would do any good, he was willing to try anything if there was even a chance of success.

Which left Rachel with the unpalatable thought that she was in Gabriel's debt. No matter how many times she tried to tell herself that he had only acted on impulse, she couldn't forget that he had asked if Hannah had had a psychological evaluation long before Dr Rigsby had suggested it.

Had it only been because he'd felt sorry for her, as Andrew had said? If what his son had said was true, he had only been amusing himself at her expense, and surely that was a more believable explanation? Hadn't she been telling herself the same thing ever since Gabriel first came into the café? Whatever he said, he couldn't think that their relationship was doomed to anything but failure.

Even so, as the bus came and she climbed aboard Rachel found herself reliving that scene in the café two weeks ago. Not that she hadn't relived it a dozen times already. The whole awful memory of it was imprinted on her mind, and whenever she closed her eyes she remembered how she had accused him of being like Joe Collins. But now she found herself trying to find excuses for herself, and justifying her words by the things he had said.

Yet all she kept coming up with was the knowledge that once again Andrew had been in the forefront of their disagreement. Gabriel had wanted to tell her why Andrew had come back to Kingsbridge and she'd refused to listen.

Well, he'd had the chance, she assured herself fiercely. He'd had the opportunity to explain the real reason for Andrew's sudden appearance, but he'd pulled back from telling her the truth. To begin with, anyway. He'd been protecting his son, she realised now, protecting him as she had tried to protect Hannah all these years. And with what success? she asked herself bitterly. Not a lot, as it had turned out.

So what was she thinking? she asked herself. That she

should have been less confrontational? Less emotional? Less willing to take Andrew's words at face value? What if it was she who had made a terrible mistake? What if Gabriel had meant what he said? Dear God, what then?

It couldn't be true, she told herself as she unlocked the café door and hurried to turn off the alarm. Just because she'd had a shock over what had happened to Hannah, she was allowing her emotions to get in the way of her common sense. Again. How many times did she have to hear something before she believed it? Gabriel didn't care about her. He *couldn't*. Apart from anything else, his family would never let him make such a mistake.

She was still arguing with herself when she picked up the phone and asked for the number of Webb's Pharmaceuticals. When she got through, the receptionist at the plant was very polite, but when Rachel asked if she could give her Gabriel's private number she was politely apologetic. She was not at liberty to give Mr Webb's private number to anyone, she said, and although Rachel identified herself, and tried to explain that she knew Mr Webb personally, the woman wouldn't be moved.

'Then perhaps you could ring Copleys and tell him I called,' Rachel suggested at last, aware that her desire to speak to Gabriel was no longer an optional thing. She wanted to speak to him, she *needed* to speak to him, and if that meant humiliating herself to this cool indifferent employee, then so be it.

'I'm afraid I don't have a number for Copleys,' replied the receptionist quellingly. 'I'm sorry, Mrs Kershaw, but—'

'Someone must have it,' exclaimed Rachel, her voice rising in concert with her frustration. 'Please. I've got to speak to him. Can't you ask someone else? The manager, perhaps?'

There was silence for a few moments, and Rachel could imagine the woman exchanging a few amused words with a fellow telephonist. Then she spoke again. 'I'll see what I can do,' she said crisply. 'Um—does Mr Webb know your number?'

'He does, but I'll give you it again,' said Rachel hurriedly, reciting the café's phone number. 'And—thank you. I do appreciate it.'

'I can't promise anything,' said the woman offhandedly, and rang off.

Rachel spent the next half-hour in a state of high tension, and by the time Stephanie turned up she was already regretting her impulsiveness. Gabriel wasn't going to phone. If he had got her message, he'd ignored it. She might just as well accept that as far as he was concerned their association was over.

'What's wrong?'

Stephanie noticed her flushed face as soon as she came in, and, rather than invent some unlikely explanation for her flustered appearance, Rachel told her what she'd done. She also told her why, relaying why Hannah's head teacher had wanted to see her and how Gabriel had played an innocent part in the little girl's progress.

'And he won't speak to you?' Stephanie frowned.

'Apparently not.' Rachel tried to sound unconcerned.

'But what did he say?'

'Oh, I haven't spoken with him,' admitted Rachel ruefully. 'I don't have his private number, so I rang the plant and asked them to give him the message.'

'And that was when?'

'Oh—nearly an hour ago.' Rachel grimaced. 'Stupid, huh?'

Stephanie shook her head. 'You don't mean that.'

'Don't I?' Rachel sniffed. 'It was a crazy idea. I mean, all right, he may have put the idea in Hannah's mind, but—'

'Stop pretending you mean that,' ordered her friend impatiently. 'Look, he may have got the message and decided to come and see you. Have you thought of that? It's not as if he's any stranger to the café.'

'Do you think so?' Rachel stared at the other woman with wide anxious eyes. 'Oh, God, and I look such a mess!'

'You look fine,' Stephanie assured her drily. 'He should be so lucky! Now, stop worrying about it and get those scones in the oven. The oven we wouldn't have if it wasn't for him, I might add. Have you forgotten that?'

Rachel gave a small smile. 'I haven't forgotten anything.'

And it was true. Just thinking about what she and Gabriel had shared caused an expanding warmth inside her that nothing could displace.

When the phone rang at half-past ten Rachel's hands were covered in flour, and Patsy, who knew nothing of what had been going on, went automatically to answer it. Her eyes widened when she heard the voice on the other end of the line, and she put her hand over the receiver as she whispered, 'It's Mr Webb, Rachel. Do you want to speak to him?'

Did she ever? Rachel nodded, frantically wiping her hands on a towel. 'Thanks, Pats,' she said, taking the handset from her, and the younger girl shrugged indifferently and went back to clearing tables.

Wishing she had more privacy than was possible at present, Rachel put the receiver to her ear and said breathily, 'Hello, Gabriel. Did you get my message?'

'It's not Gabriel, Rachel,' said a harsh amused voice. 'It's Andrew. Sorry to disappoint you, babe, but the old man's not here.'

Rachel's heart sank. 'I see.'

'Yeah.' Andrew sounded smug. 'It was quite a surprise when I got your message from the receptionist at Webb's. I gather my father wasn't fool enough to give you his private number. I just wonder what you think you've got to gain by pursuing him like this.'

Rachel gasped. 'I'm not pursuing him.'

'No?' Andrew sounded sceptical. 'Well, why are you ringing him here, then? The guy's given you the brush-off, for God's sake. What part of that don't you understand?'

Rachel wanted to ask, *Is that what he said?* But she didn't have the courage. 'I just wanted to speak to him,' she insisted. 'Will you tell him I called?'

'He's not here at Copleys,' said Andrew flatly. 'As far as I know he's in Siena. Italy, that is. There's a woman there my grandmother wants him to meet. He and Nonna flew out on Friday night.'

Rachel hung up then. It wasn't that she entirely believed the bit about the woman his mother wanted him to meet, but if Gabriel was out of the country she was wasting her time. Andrew would never pass her message on to his father. Whatever feelings he had ever had for her had been destroyed long before he found her and Gabriel in bed together.

Where before she had been flushed and excited, now she was pale and drawn, and Stephanie, who had made herself scarce while Rachel was taking the call, gave an impatient exclamation.

'What did he say, for God's sake?'

'He didn't,' said Rachel, turning away to wash her hands at the sink. 'It wasn't—Gabriel. It was Andrew. Gabriel's not there. He's in Italy, with his mother.'

Stephanie frowned. 'I see.' She hesitated. 'So you'll phone him when he gets back?'

'No.' Rachel swallowed. 'I don't know the number, remember? Besides, according to Andrew, his father has given me the brush-off.'

'Since when did you believe anything Andrew Webb said?' asked Stephanie shortly, picking up the phone. With nimble fingers she dialled 1471, and waited while the automated voice gave her the number of who'd been calling. Scribbling it on her order pad, she handed it to Rachel. 'There you are. That's the number you want. And stop looking so shattered. Andrew's jealous, that's all. Who wouldn't be? He tried hard enough, God knows!'

Rachel took the sheet of paper and gave a shaky laugh. 'You're so good for my ego.'

'No, I'm practical, is all,' said Stephanie drily. 'Now, I'm not saying that that number is the answer to all your problems, but at least if you do decide to ring Copleys again you don't have to go through some snotty receptionist.'

'Thanks.' Rachel folded the sheet and put it into her skirt pocket. Then she bestowed a kiss on her friend's cheek. 'You're a pal.'

She told her mother what she'd done that evening. She felt the other woman deserved to know what she was thinking, and for once Mrs Redfern didn't start grumbling as soon as Rachel mentioned Gabriel's name.

'I suppose he deserves to know,' she admitted grudgingly. 'If you think he'll be interested, that is. But I doubt if he'll get in touch with you. I'd heard he'd gone back to London, and if you say he's in Italy—well, I expect he'll be thinking of taking up the reins of the company again when he gets back.'

'Mmm.'

Rachel didn't trust herself to make any comment. The idea that Gabriel might not come back to Kingsbridge at all was too upsetting to think about. Wasn't it too soon for him to be thinking of resuming his duties as CEO of Webb's Pharmaceuticals in any case? What if he collapsed again? What if she knew nothing about it? God, how was she going to survive not knowing where he was or what he was doing?

Dr Williams rang on Wednesday evening to let Rachel know that an appointment had been made for Hannah to see the child psychologist the following week, and on Thursday Mrs Redfern reported that the physiotherapist, Mrs Stone, had noticed significant improvement in the little girl's mobility. It was as if now that Hannah had decided to walk again her progress was accelerating, and Rachel buried her own unhappiness over Gabriel in the fierce pride she felt for her daughter. This was what was important to her, she told herself. Nothing else should even come close.

But it did.

In spite of what Andrew had told her, and Gabriel's continuing silence, hope sprang eternal. Every morning she suffered the quivering expectation of wondering if this might be the day when she'd see Gabriel again, and every night she felt the bitterness of knowing that once again her hopes had been dashed. Day followed day with depressing familiarity, but no dark-haired stranger came into the café, no deep sensual tones called her to the phone. As Andrew had so smugly told her, Gabriel wanted nothing more to do with her, and somehow she had to stop thinking that he did.

And then, on Friday evening, the phone rang as she was about to leave the café.

She was late, and, expecting it to be her mother, Rachel lifted the receiver with mild impatience. She was wondering what it was that couldn't wait until she got home, and then was almost shocked out of her mind when an achingly familiar voice said, 'Rachel?'

Trembling, she groped for the edge of the counter and supported herself against it. 'Gabriel?' she breathed, almost disbelievingly. 'Oh, God, is that really you?'

'Who were you expecting?' he enquired coolly, and she blessed whatever fate had decreed that on this particular evening she should be a few minutes late in leaving.

'I—nobody,' she denied weakly. 'Um—did you get my message?'

'Your message?' Plainly, he hadn't. 'No. I got no message. When did you leave one?'

Rachel was shaking so badly she could hardly stand.

'I—I tried to ring you on Monday morning,' she said tremulously. 'I didn't have your number, so I rang the plant and asked the receptionist if it was possible to get in touch with you. I wanted to tell you about Hannah. She's been getting out of her chair on her own, and a week ago her head teacher called me into the school to ask if I knew anything about it. Of course I didn't. As far as I was concerned she was still totally paralysed, but it's not true. There's been a distinct improvement, and if she hadn't fallen trying to pick up a paintbrush we might still have known nothing about it.'

The words had come bubbling out of her mouth, as much the result of nervousness as anything, and she knew they weren't exactly coherent. All the same, when he didn't immediately answer her, she realised how foolish she must sound. What reason did she have for thinking he was still interested in their lives? He hadn't had her message. That wasn't why he'd rung. For all she knew he might have something entirely different on his mind.

'Anyway,' she said, hurrying to fill the awkward silence that had fallen, 'you didn't ring me to talk about Hannah.' She paused. 'How—how are you? Andrew told me you were in Italy. Did you have a good—?'

'*Andrew!*' Gabriel's interjection was raw. 'You admit you've spoken to Andrew?' He paused. 'Have you seen him?'

'No.' Rachel was indignant. 'Of course I haven't *seen* him. Why would I? I told you, I tried to get in touch with you by ringing the plant and—'

'Yes, yes.' Gabriel spoke impatiently. 'But where does Andrew come into this? Why did you ring him?'

'I didn't ring him.' Rachel's voice grew defensive in response to the accusation in his. 'He—he took the message.'

'Where? At the plant?' Gabriel sounded sceptical and she wanted to scream with frustration. 'Andrew never goes to the plant.'

'Not at the plant.' Rachel felt a painful lump in her throat. Here they were arguing about Andrew again, and she didn't know how it had happened. 'He rang me from Copleys. The receptionist I spoke to must have passed my message on to him.'

There was another of those pregnant silences and Rachel wondered what he was thinking. He couldn't possibly believe that she'd speak to Andrew voluntarily. Or was she being hopelessly naïve in thinking that she and Gabriel might take up where they'd left off?

'And your story is that you rang to tell me about Hannah?' he said at last, and Rachel gave a startled gasp.

'My story?' she echoed. 'It's no story. It's the truth.' She took a gulp of air, and then continued tightly, 'I realise it was probably silly to think that you'd want to know—that you'd even be interested. I'm sorry, but it seemed a good idea at the time.'

'Don't be stupid!' Gabriel's voice was harsh with emphasis. 'Of course I'm interested in Hannah. Dammit, that was why I was ringing you. Despite what—well, despite what I thought, I didn't think that child deserved to suffer just because her mother wouldn't listen to reason.'

'Thanks.'

Rachel pressed her lips together before she could say anything more. The urge to ask him what he meant by criticising her when he hadn't demurred from discussing their relationship with his son was almost irresistible, but this wasn't about her. As he'd just said, it was about Hannah. And he was right: her daughter did deserve better.

'And I'm glad that she's making progress at last,' he added, and for the first time there was a trace of warmth in his tone. 'How does she feel about it?'

'Good.' Rachel didn't know how long she could go on without losing control. 'She's going to see a child psychologist next week. Just as you suggested.'

'Great.' He was evidently pleased. 'How do you feel about that?'

'As you pointed out earlier, my feelings aren't in question here,' said Rachel stiffly. 'But, as you'd expect, I'm delighted, too.'

'You don't sound delighted.'

'Well, I am.' Rachel was having a struggle to keep the emotion out of her voice. 'I—I did want to thank you, actually. For what you did. If Hannah hadn't been so excited by your horses she might never have found the courage to try and stand by herself.'

'You think it was crucial?' He was cynical.

'I do.' And, in an effort to justify that belief, she added swiftly, 'She's determined to learn to ride herself. I think your groom, Katy something-or-other, gave her the idea, and she can't wait to—to—try it.'

But her last words were reluctant. Once again her tongue had run away with her, and she realised with a feeling of dismay how what she'd said might be interpreted. God, he was going to think she was asking if Hannah could visit Copleys again, when that was the last thing he'd have in mind.

'I mean,' she appended unhappily, 'when she grows up, of course. And by then, please God, she'll have the full use of her legs.'

'I'm sure she will.' Gabriel's voice was terse now. 'Hannah's a determined little girl.' He paused. 'Like her mother.'

Rachel didn't answer him. She couldn't. The change of topic was too upsetting for her fragile emotional state, and now all she wanted to do was put the receiver down and forget he'd ever made this call.

'I—I'll tell Hannah you rang,' she got out at last, but before she could hang up the phone, Gabriel uttered a strangled sound.

'God,' he said savagely, 'can't we talk about anything else but Hannah?'

Rachel struggled to keep her tears at bay. 'I—I thought that was what you—what you—'

'Wanted?' he demanded, breaking into her trembling words. 'Well, it wasn't.' He gave another anguished moan. 'Oh, that was my excuse for ringing you, yes, but dammit, Rachel, it's you I wanted—I *needed* to talk to. Talk to me, can't you? Haven't you missed me at all?'

Rachel held the phone away from her ear for a moment,

staring at it as if she couldn't believe what she was hearing. And then, jamming it back again, she countered unsteadily, 'Have you missed me?'

'Do you have to ask?' Gabriel spoke almost bitterly. 'Will I damn myself completely if I tell you I've thought of nothing else but you ever since I walked out of the café three weeks ago?'

A sob escaped her. She couldn't help it. It was such a relief hearing him say what she had so desperately wanted to hear, and tears were suddenly pouring down her cheeks.

'Oh, Gabriel,' she breathed, licking the salty droplets from her lips. 'Do you mean it?'

'I don't usually say things I don't mean,' he retorted huskily, and she gave a tremulous little laugh.

'You said you didn't think I cared about anybody,' she reminded him unsteadily, and he groaned.

'I did say I didn't *usually* say things I don't mean,' he admitted ruefully. 'Even I've been known to say stupid things on occasion. Particularly where you're concerned, as it happens. Do you forgive me?'

'Do you forgive *me*?' she responded huskily, and at last Gabriel seemed to detect the emotion in her voice.

'Are you crying?' he exclaimed, and when she didn't answer, he continued, 'I'm coming to pick you up. Give me five minutes and I'll be outside the café.'

'Five minutes?' Rachel was horrified. 'You'll kill yourself!'

'Only if I run into something coming out of the Golden Lion's car park,' remarked Gabriel drily. 'I've been here all afternoon, trying to pluck up the courage to cross the street.'

'You haven't!' Rachel caught her breath. 'But why?'

'I'll tell you when I see you,' he promised softly. 'Get your coat. It's raining outside.'

CHAPTER FOURTEEN

By the time the Mercedes drew to a stop outside, Rachel had phoned her mother to tell her she'd be late—though not why—made sure the power had been turned off, the alarm was activated and the door locked. She was hovering under the overhang that shaded the café's window when the big car cruised up to the kerb, and her eyes widened in surprise when she saw Gabriel himself at the wheel.

'Get in,' he said, leaning across the passenger seat to thrust the door open, and, squashing any lingering doubts she might have had, Rachel scooted across the pavement and into the car.

Because it was a no-parking area—and the start of the rush hour—Gabriel was forced to drive on at once, and he spared her only a passing glance before moving into the press of traffic. His attention had to be concentrated on avoiding the many obstacles that blocked the one-way street, and Rachel gripped her handbag tightly in her lap as he wove around jaywalking pedestrians and illegally parked vehicles.

But, although she determinedly watched the road ahead, Rachel was intensely conscious of him beside her. The fleeting glance he had cast her way had been enough for her to see that wherever he'd been it hadn't done much for his health. He looked pale—gaunt, even—the deep grooves she had first noticed bracketing his mouth back in evidence. He looked older, too, and her heart ached at the thought that she might be responsible for even a part of his appearance.

'Sorry about this,' he said abruptly, as if he thought she was blaming him for the traffic snarl-up. It was true, she was sitting rather stiffly in her seat, and she had made no attempt to say anything since she got into the car.

'It's not your fault,' she murmured now, glancing his way for the first time. 'How—how are you? Really?'

Gabriel's lips twisted. 'How do I look?' And, when Rachel didn't immediately answer him, 'That bad, huh?' He gave a short laugh. 'At least I can rely on you to tell me the truth.'

Rachel sighed. 'You look—tired, that's all,' she protested quickly. 'Have you started work again?'

'Not yet.' His voice was flat. 'As Andrew told you, I did go to Italy for a few days. I accompanied my mother home, as a matter of fact. She hates flying alone.'

Rachel swallowed. 'What—what did Andrew tell you about me?'

Gabriel didn't immediately answer her. He appeared to be involved with steering the big car out of the narrow street where the café was situated and into the broader thoroughfare that led to the outskirts of the small town, but Rachel sensed his mind wasn't wholly on his driving. She knew him so well, she thought; or at least she believed she did. There was more to this than he had admitted thus far, and her stomach clenched at the prospect of confronting more of Andrew's lies; or maybe confronting Andrew himself.

'Do you mind if we wait until we get where we're going before we talk about Andrew?' he asked at last. 'There's something I've got to tell you about him and I'd prefer not to be gripping a steering wheel at the time.'

'Well, where are we going?' she asked. But she knew. This was the way to Copleys. She might only have been there a couple of times, but she knew the route by heart.

'If you don't mind, I thought we'd go to my house,' he responded, as she'd known he would, and her nerves tightened again at the realisation that her instincts were as sharp as ever.

'Did—did he tell you he'd seen me?' she demanded abruptly, unable to wait so coolly for him to tell her the worst. 'Did you believe him?'

Gabriel sighed. 'Rachel—'

'Did you or didn't you—?' She broke off, and then added chokingly, 'Was that really why you rang?'

'I wanted to speak to you about Hannah,' he replied doggedly. 'I told you that.'

Rachel's nails dug into her palms as she turned to look at him. 'And that was why you sat in the Golden Lion all afternoon? Because you wanted to ask me about Hannah?'

Gabriel groaned. 'All right, no,' he admitted harshly. 'Hannah was only an excuse. Of course I'm delighted to hear that her prognosis is so much more optimistic, but—God, Rachel, it's you I wanted to see. You know that.'

Rachel trembled. 'So why didn't you come into the café?'

'You know why,' he muttered, swinging the wheel, and she suddenly realised they were about to turn into the gates of Copleys.

'Do I?' she countered, aware that this was her last chance to talk to him on her own ground, so to speak. 'Stop the car, Gabriel. I want to know exactly what Andrew said.'

She thought he wasn't going to obey her. The gates had already swung open, and for a second his foot seemed to press even harder on the accelerator. But then, with a muffled oath, he stood on the brake, and the powerful car came to a shuddering halt.

The silence in the car after the engine had been turned off was deafening, and Rachel wondered at her own audacity in ordering him to do anything. But then her courage asserted itself, and, licking her dry lips, she said, 'He did say something, didn't he? And you believed him!'

Gabriel's shoulders sagged. 'Okay,' he said flatly. 'I did believe him. At first, anyway.' His eyes darkened. 'You believed him, too, didn't you? That night—that night we were together? You're not going to pretend it was our lovemaking that sent you fleeing out into the night without even letting me ask Mario to drive you home?'

Rachel felt a trace of colour enter her cheeks. 'That was different,' she said defensively, and Gabriel's mouth twisted.

'How different?' he asked huskily. 'You wouldn't even allow me to explain why he was there. On three separate occasions.'

'Three?'

'Sure.' His eyes gleamed in his pale face, dark and irresistibly appealing. 'And if you hadn't believed that garbage he spouted about me feeling sorry for you we wouldn't be in this position now.'

'That may be true—'

'It is true.' Gabriel expelled a weary breath. 'Look, there's something you need to know about Andrew. The reason why I had to go to London a few weeks ago was because he had been arrested for drug dealing. He needed my help to get a lawyer, to invent an adequate defence for what he'd done.'

Rachel's lips parted. 'Oh.'

'Yes, oh!' said Gabriel drily. 'In his defence, I have to say his arrest was somewhat premature. He wasn't dealing in drugs, but he had got hooked up with someone who was and it was all a bit messy.'

'And that's why he came back to Copleys?'

'No.' Gabriel chose his words with care. 'You may remember I had a phone call that evening we went out to dinner? It was from Andrew. He needed money, more money, and I refused to give it to him. I'd told him I wasn't going to support his habit and I guess he'd decided that he might have more luck if he spoke to me face-to-face. Finding us together must have been a hell of a shock, but that doesn't excuse his behaviour—even if it does provide a reason for it.'

Rachel shook her head. 'I had no idea.'

'No.' Gabriel conceded the point. 'But perhaps you can understand why I was so reluctant to tell you. Whatever his faults, he is my son.' He paused. 'Can you understand?'

'I can understand your feelings,' said Rachel slowly. 'But I'd like to know what he told you about my call. He did tell you I'd phoned, didn't he? I mean, the receptionist at the plant can confirm it.'

'Yes. He told me you'd phoned.' Gabriel's hands tightened on the wheel. 'He said you'd wanted to talk to him.'

'To him?' Rachel was horrified. 'But why?'

'Why do you think? For old times' sake? Because it was good to see him again? Because you wished you and he had never broken up?'

'No!'

'No, well, I have to say I found it bloody hard to believe.'

'But you did believe it?' Rachel stared at him.

'Initially, I suppose. If I'm honest, I'll say that it was what I'd expected, what I'd anticipated might happen. I mean—' this as Rachel stared at him with incredulous eyes '—I've always thought I was too old for you, and Andrew was only saying what I'd secretly believed myself. He is my son, as I say. There must have been aspects of him that attracted you to me—'

'No!' Rachel couldn't listen to any more of this. Turning in her seat, she grasped Gabriel's face between her two palms and turned him towards her. 'Andrew's—not—half—the—man—you—are,' she cried fiercely, interspersing her words with eager kisses that ranged from his temple to his cheeks and finally reached his mouth. 'You're nothing like Andrew,' she added unsteadily, and this time when she kissed him Gabriel didn't resist.

'Are you sure?' he demanded against her lips, and her answer was to wind her arms around his neck and meet his searching tongue with her own.

'Try me,' she breathed invitingly, and Gabriel released her mouth to bury his face in the hollow of her neck.

'I intend to,' he whispered softly, 'but not with my security guard watching us on his monitor.' He released her and slid his fingers through her hair, looping it back behind her ears. 'Hold that thought,' he added, and she coloured in sudden understanding. 'Don't go cold on me now.'

'I don't think I could,' said Rachel with devastating honesty, her hand sliding intimately over his thigh, and earned herself a look that was full of frustration and promise.

'Say anything more like that and I may decide not to take the risk,' he replied hoarsely. Starting the car, he imprisoned her hand against his leg. 'Thank God my mother's gone home. I don't think I'd have the patience to deal with explanations right now. There'll be plenty of time for that.'

Rachel withdrew her hand, suddenly apprehensive again. 'And Andrew?'

'Andrew's in London,' said Gabriel wryly. 'Or that's where he's supposed to be. He left here when I did.'

'Oh, but he couldn't have.' Rachel didn't hesitate before rummaging in her bag and bringing out the scrap of paper with the phone number Stephanie had retrieved on it. 'When he phoned me he said he was at Copleys. He said you weren't there, as I told you, but after he'd rung off I—we—dialled the automatic recall number so that if—if I wanted to ring you again I'd have your number. Isn't this it?'

Gabriel brought the car to an abrupt halt before the house and took the slip of paper from her. He read it, and then said grimly, 'This is Andrew's mobile number.' He shook his head. 'He rang you from London, not Copleys.'

Rachel caught her breath. 'So if I'd used the number—'

'You'd have got Andrew,' agreed Gabriel harshly. 'Which would have gone a long way to confirming his story.'

'But he couldn't have known I'd take the number!'

'Do you want to bet?' Gabriel sighed. 'God, Rachel, that selfish young fool has a lot to answer for.'

Rachel stared at him, tempted to tell him about the lies Andrew had told her, but she didn't. 'He's jealous,' she said instead, realising that what Stephanie had said was true. She glanced towards the house. 'Are you going to invite me in?'

Some time later Rachel stood in Gabriel's shower cubicle, allowing tepid water to cool her burning flesh. Although the walls of the cubicle weren't mirrored, she could plainly see her image in the cream tiles, and there was no mistaking the rosy glow that tinged her skin.

And why not? she thought incredulously. For the past hour she had been in Gabriel's arms, in Gabriel's bed, making mad passionate love on Gabriel's soft cotton sheets. They had been hungry for one another and, although they'd eventually got around to taking off all their clothes, to begin with there had only been time to peel the necessary garments aside and give in to the urgent needs that had refused to be denied.

Rachel felt a smile lift her lips. For a man who had looked so old and drawn when she'd first seen him Gabriel had proved remarkably resilient. When she'd left him a few moments ago there'd been little sign of the weary fatigue that had dogged his features earlier. Being with her again, making love with her again, had performed a minor miracle, and Rachel knew a spreading warmth inside her at the knowledge that she, and she alone, could do that for him.

Closing her eyes, she luxuriated in the cooling spray, and then almost jumped out of her skin when firm hands descended on her hips, drawing her back against a warm familiar body.

'You were taking too long,' said Gabriel huskily, nuzzling her shoulder. 'I thought I'd come and help you.'

Rachel's legs felt weak. 'You want to help me?'

'Do I ever?' he conceded, reaching for the shower gel and pouring some into his palm. Then, after rubbing both hands together, he slid his palms down her thighs in a sleek sensuous motion. 'What do you think?'

Rachel sagged against him and was immediately aware that she wasn't the only one of them that was more than half aroused. The pulsating heat of his erection throbbed against her bottom, and she groped behind her to take his fullness into her hand.

'God, Rachel,' he groaned, giving up his sensual massage of her legs to remove her hand from his body. 'I want you again. I can't seem to get enough of you.' He uttered a choked sound. 'Now isn't that an admission to make?'

'I don't mind,' she whispered achingly, as his hands sought the swollen fullness of her breasts. She twisted in his arms. 'If you let me go, I'll get dried.'

'Why bother?' asked Gabriel, looking down at her with dark disturbing eyes. 'I'm only going to make you wet again.'

Rachel caught her breath. 'We can't,' she protested, when she realised what he really meant, and Gabriel's lips formed a small smile.

'Of course we can,' he assured her, lifting one of her legs and trapping it at his waist. 'It's as easy as you want it to be.'

And it was. With the wall of the shower against her back, Gabriel slid slickly into her, and she wound her arms around his neck and her legs about his hips.

The sensation was incredible. With the shower still spilling its warmth around them, Gabriel moved slowly and insistently towards his goal. He seemed intent on wringing every last shred of erotic emotion from the experience, and Rachel pressed her head back against the wall, sobbing her need without inhibition.

It was over far too soon. Despite Gabriel's efforts to prolong their excitement Rachel's climax couldn't be denied, and she felt his shuddering release overtake hers.

'God, I love you,' he muttered, allowing her legs to slide to the floor, and she allowed him to leave her with real reluctance.

'I—love you, too,' she said helplessly, and knew that whatever the future held this man was going to be a part of it.

'And now I suppose I'm going to have to go and face your mother again,' he remarked drily, after he had satisfactorily shown his pleasure at that announcement, and Rachel belatedly remembered that that was why she'd gone to take a shower in the first place.

'Do you mind?' she asked, looking up at him with anxious eyes, and Gabriel gave a disarming smile.

'My darling, when you look at me like that, anything you ask is worthwhile,' he assured her softly. 'And, after all, she is going to be my mother-in-law, isn't she?'

Rachel caught her breath. 'Is she?'

His eyes darkened. 'Well, isn't she?'

'I—suppose so,' she said breathlessly. 'If you'll have me.'

EPILOGUE

RACHEL and Gabriel's first child was born nine months later. And Gabriel was at his wife's bedside when his lusty second son came into the world. At eight pounds, ten ounces, and with a mass of dark hair, the baby was the image of his father, and Rachel thought how lucky she was to have two such attractive males in her life.

Hannah loved the baby on sight. For years she had envied friends who had younger or older brothers and sisters, and her first question when Rachel was up and about again was to ask if they could have a baby girl next time.

'We'll see,' said her stepfather drily, drawing the little girl onto his lap. 'But I think we should let your mother get used to having two children before we give her three, don't you?'

'Indeed we should,' agreed Rachel's mother, who had been staying at Copleys to look after her granddaughter while Rachel was recovering her strength. 'Besides, since you started walking yourself, we never know where you are.'

Hannah looked smug. 'Well, I'm usually at the stables,' she admitted thoughtfully. 'Do you know, Katy says I'm going to make a good rider?' She frowned. 'One of these days, anyway.'

'So long as you don't do anything silly,' put in Mrs Redfern, before Rachel could respond. 'And now come along. I think we should go and find Joseph and let your mother and father have a few minutes to themselves. Having a baby can be a tiring thing. Your mother needs to rest.'

Hannah followed her grandmother obediently out of the room, with only a fleeting backward glance for her parents. Rachel guessed she was already estimating how long she need stay with the older woman before she could escape to the stables again. She and Katy had become firm friends, and Rachel knew she could trust the young groom to keep a weather eye on her daughter.

Gabriel got up from the chair he had been occupying as soon as the others left the room. He came to stand looking down at his wife, who was reclining on one of the soft leather sofas in the drawing room at Copleys.

'Is your mother right?' he asked concernedly, coming down on his haunches beside her and taking one of her hands to his lips. 'Are you tired? It has been only a few days. Shouldn't you still be in bed?'

'I'm fine,' Rachel assured him, although having their son had been an exhausting experience. 'Don't you know some women have their babies and then get up and do a day's work?'

'I trust you're not planning on going back to work in the near future?' Gabriel responded warningly. 'I'm hoping I'll have you to myself for a few more weeks yet.'

'No.' Rachel smiled. 'Stephanie can hold the fort for as long as necessary. As a matter of fact, I think she likes being in charge. It's a new experience for her.'

'Good.' Gabriel eased onto the sofa beside her, his hip warm against her thigh. 'Because I was wondering how you'd feel about spending a few days in London next week. I've got some meetings I can't avoid, and you know I don't like leaving you behind.'

Ever since he and Rachel had got married Gabriel had commuted between Kingsbridge and London, only going into the city when his business commitments couldn't be conducted by phone, fax, or via the Internet. Like Rachel, he had learned to delegate, and Rachel was making sure he didn't get the chance to overwork again.

'But what about—?'

'Our son?' Gabriel grinned. 'We really will have to choose a name for him.' He paused. 'We'll take him with us, of course. Hannah, too, if she can drag herself away from the horses.'

Rachel leant forward and rested her cheek against his shoulder. She was so lucky, she thought contentedly. She had a daughter who could now walk again, a darling baby son, and the best and most thoughtful husband in the world.

The last nine months hadn't been without incident, however.

First there had been the results of Hannah's examination by the psychologist to deal with. Under hypnosis, the little girl had initially become quite hysterical, and it had taken a great deal of care and patience to calm her fears. But Dr Matthews was an expert in his field, and over a period of weeks he had eventually discovered what he believed to be the reason for Hannah's self-imposed paralysis.

Rachel had been shocked to learn that Larry had been planning to leave her and take Hannah with him. He had apparently been talking about it just before the accident. Dr Matthews believed that because the child hadn't known her father had been killed in the crash she had lost the use of her legs deliberately, believing that if she couldn't walk she couldn't get into a car and he couldn't take her with him.

There was much more to it than that, of course, but Rachel had been stunned by these revelations. She had known she and Larry were having problems, but she hadn't suspected that there might be someone else. Dr Matthews had said Hannah had talked about her father telling her she was going to get a new mother. Rachel was left with the belated knowledge that one of the women from the insurance office where Larry had worked, and who had attended his funeral, had probably had more to grieve about than she had.

Gabriel had been a tower of strength all the time Hannah was attending the clinic, and he'd understood that Rachel had things to work through, too. He hadn't insisted on seeing her, or pressured her in any way, and she had been grateful for his understanding.

But gradually Hannah's progress and her own eagerness
to be with him had overcome all obstacles, and by the time
she'd discovered she was pregnant they were already making
arrangements for their wedding.

Arrangements which had had to be accelerated, she remembered now, nestling closer as Gabriel's hand came to
massage the nape of her neck. They had been planning an
October wedding, but in the event they'd been married at the
end of August, with Hannah as bridesmaid, struggling
proudly down the aisle of the local church on her newly
acquired crutches.

Gabriel's mother and some of his aunts and uncles and
cousins had attended the wedding, and Rachel had had her
first experience of what it was like to be part of a large Italian
family. Signora Webb had been particularly effusive, and although Rachel doubted her baby son would ever hold the
same place in his grandmother's heart as Andrew did, the
older woman was delighted to know that *her* son was now
happy at last.

Andrew had not attended the wedding, but at Christmas
he had turned up at Copleys with presents for his new family.
Ironically enough, he'd seemed to get on really well with
Hannah, and she'd accepted him as her new *older* brother
without a problem. Rachel knew it would be some time before she was prepared to totally trust him again, but time was
a great healer and hopefully they all had plenty of that.

Hannah had been walking properly since Christmas, when
she'd thrown her crutches away. And, to celebrate, Gabriel
had bought her a pony of her own.

They had called the foal that had first started Hannah on
her road to recovery Phoenix, but now he was too big for
her to look after. Even so, she always made a point of going
to see him every time she went down to the stable yard, and
Gabriel was of the opinion that in a couple of years, when
the pony became too small, Hannah would be able to ride
Phoenix instead.

'What do you think of Jared?' Rachel murmured now, turning her mouth against the warm brown skin of Gabriel's throat, and felt his lips brush the top of her head.

'Jared who?' he asked huskily, and she slid a possessive hand over his thigh.

'Jared Webb,' she said impatiently. 'Our son. I think Jared is a nice name, don't you?'

Gabriel drew back to cradle her face between his palms. 'It sounds good to me,' he said equably. 'But do you think we could insert Benedict in there somewhere? Benedict was my father's name.'

'Jared Benedict Webb,' tried Rachel consideringly. 'J.B. Webb. Yes, that sounds pretty good, doesn't it?'

'Jared it is, then,' said Gabriel softly. 'Jared and Hannah. Yes, they sound good together.'

'*Andrew*, Jared and Hannah,' Rachel corrected him gently. 'We have so much. We can't leave him out.'

'You're a very special woman, Rachel Webb,' Gabriel told her, bestowing a warm kiss at the corner of her soft mouth. 'Okay, I know he's kicked his drug habit, and he's making a real effort to learn about the business, but I hope he realises how lucky he is.'

'So long as you do,' Rachel murmured teasingly, linking her arms about his neck. 'That's good enough for me.'

And as Gabriel bore her back against the cushions and proceeded to show her that he did, she was content.

If you enjoyed what you just read,
then we've got an offer you can't resist!

Take 2 bestselling
love stories FREE!

Plus get a FREE surprise gift!

HARLEQUIN Presents

**The world's bestselling romance series.
Seduction and passion guaranteed!**

**Pick up a Harlequin Presents® novel and you will
enter a world of spine-tingling passion and
provocative, tantalizing romance!**

Join us in 2002 for an exciting selection of titles
from all your favorite authors:

Red Hot Revenge
COLE CAMERON'S REVENGE #2223, January
by Sandra Marton

Secret Passions
A truly thrilling new duet
THE SECRET VENGEANCE #2236, March
THE SECRET LOVE CHILD #2242, April
by Miranda Lee

A Mediterranean Marriage
THE BELLINI BRIDE #2224, January
by Michelle Reid
and
THE ITALIAN'S WIFE #2235, March
by Lynne Graham

An upbeat, contemporary story
THE CITY-GIRL BRIDE #2229, February
by Penny Jordan

An involving and dramatic read
A RICH MAN'S TOUCH #2230, February
by Anne Mather

On sale in the New Year
Available wherever Harlequin Books are sold.

HARLEQUIN®
Makes any time special ®

Visit us at www.eHarlequin.com

HPDECPRE

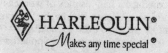

Coming Next Month

HARLEQUIN *Presents*

THE BEST HAS JUST GOTTEN BETTER!

#2235 THE ITALIAN'S WIFE Lynne Graham

Rio Lombardi, managing director of Lombardi Industries, has an outburst of conscience. He insists that Holly, a homeless single mother, stay at his luxurious home. Rio then proceeds to lavish her and her baby with all that money can buy. But his emotions are caught off guard....

#2236 THE SECRET VENGEANCE Miranda Lee

While searching for his father's mistress, Luke Freeman has information that leads him to Celia. This beautiful young woman is not who he's looking for—but he has to have her all the same....

#2237 A WHIRLWIND MARRIAGE Helen Brooks

Marianne's marriage to Zeke Buchanan had been blissfully happy until recently—now somehow she had the feeling she was losing him.... Had they married too soon, too impulsively? Marianne was determined to fight to keep her husband's love!

#2238 THE BILLIONAIRE AFFAIR Diana Hamilton

Powerful businessman Ben Dexter had forgone a wife and family for years, ever since Caroline Harvey had betrayed him. But now it was time to get her out of his system. He would find her, indulge in an affair with her—and then get on with his life....

#2239 THE MISTRESS'S CHILD Sharon Kendrick

Lisi has never told Philip Caprice that their evening of passion resulted in a baby—until now. Philip's solution is that Lisi and their son move in with him—but is he only playing at happy families?

#2240 ROME'S REVENGE Sara Craven

Rome d'Angelo could have had his pick of women—only, his fiancée had already been chosen for him, by his grandfather. A family feud meant Rome was forced to make Cory Grant his bride and then jilt her. But his plans were spoiled when he discovered that he genuinely liked Cory....